*Tales of the Were ~ Redstone Clan*

# Red

BIANCA D'ARC

Copyright © 2013 Bianca D'Arc
Cover Art by Valerie Tibbs

ISBN: 1493657798
ISBN-13: 978-1493657797

# DEDICATION

This one goes out to my incredible team of helper elves. First and foremost, cover artist, Valerie Tibbs. She puts up with me and somehow manages to WOW me with each new cover she creates for my babies. Thank you, V, from the bottom of my heart.

I'd also like to thank the lovely Michelle Boone and Peggy McChesney, who were kind enough to help with last-minute details.

Many thanks also to my editor, Heidi, and the fantastic readers who send encouragement and love to me via facebook, my group and email. You guys ROCK! And let me not forget the awesome folks I've met at this year's cons, including the "bitches" and all those who joined me in "doing the dragon" at RAW 2013. That's a memory I will never forget.

And, as always, to my family. I couldn't live this life—a life I dreamed of—without their love and support. I love you guys!

# CHAPTER ONE

"Hey, Red! How's it hanging?"

"Damn. I knew I shouldn't have answered the phone." Steve Redstone's smile belied his gruff tone. The call was from one of his oldest and best Army buddies—Derek "Deke" Morrow—an entirely human soldier, but a great guy nonetheless. He was also one of the most skilled warriors Steve had ever known.

"Man, I've got a big favor to ask you." Deke's tone was serious and Steve sobered.

"Spill, bro. You know I'll do what I can for you."

"Thanks, man. Knew I could count on you. Thing is, my baby sister is heading your way. One of her girlfriends decided it would be fun to have her bachelorette party in Sin City. It's not that I don't trust Trish, as much as I don't trust her friends. This is an accident waiting to happen and I need some backup. I can't go. She'd kill me if I showed my face, but she doesn't know you and you're local."

"So you want me to show her a good time?" Steve relaxed. Babysitting, he could do. Teasing his friend just came naturally.

"You do, and I'll break both your legs." The tone said Deke was only half-joking.

"Relax. I've got you covered. What hotel are they staying

1

at?"

A few minutes later, the call ended and Steve had all the information he'd need to track down his good friend's wayward sister. He'd establish surveillance first. Check the lay of the land and see what kind of mischief the girls were getting up to. If necessary, he could call on some members of his Clan to help him keep an eye on things, but he didn't really think that would be necessary. How much trouble could a few young human girls get into, after all?

Steve cursed himself for even thinking that a few hours later as he leaned against the wall of a dark club, watching the half-dozen women who had stormed the Las Vegas strip with the way-too-gorgeous little sister of his friend. Trisha Morrow was a knockout. That was something Steve hadn't counted on.

When Derek talked about his kid sister, he always made her sound like a teenager. The woman currently knocking back an entire row of colorful, questionable test tube shots at the bar was no teenager. Far from it. She was an adult and as lovely as her brother was deadly.

Steve's first sight of her had nearly knocked him off his feet, and his reaction hadn't tamed any in the two hours since. He'd followed the gaggle of women out of the hotel where they were staying and tailed them to this club. They were enjoying the live band, some dancing and a whole lot of drinking. Too much drinking, by his standards. Some of the girls were getting sloppy drunk, but Trisha Morrow seemed to be able to hold her liquor with a little more dignity than her friends. That was something, at least.

He knew she was just as shitfaced as the other women though. She was unsteady on those sexy high heels and the way her short skirt rode up when she tried to get on the barstool had nearly given him a heart attack. She was tall for a human woman. Just a little shorter than her brother, who was about six foot. Trish had to be about five-nine or so. A nice height to match Steve's six-foot-two.

And he really shouldn't be thinking thoughts like that. No, not at all. Her brother would kill him if he even *thought* Steve was thinking about his little sister in an inappropriate way. It would end a friendship Steve valued, and he wasn't willing to give up that relationship over a woman. Even a woman as knock-out gorgeous as Trisha Morrow.

Steve kept watch from afar. He didn't want to know her scent. He stayed well upwind so he wouldn't accidentally smell the sexy, feminine aroma he just knew would rev his engine to full throttle. It was bad enough seeing her. He didn't want to know the intimate details her scent would reveal to him.

If he wanted to keep his friend, it was better he didn't know. Even though his inner cougar clawed at his insides to learn more about the pretty female. The cat appreciated Trisha's beauty and its innate curiosity pushed at Steve to find out more about her, but he couldn't. He was a babysitter. That's it.

Steve was so busy watching the woman and thinking about how he mustn't get too close to her that he almost missed the danger when it struck. One of Trisha's friends—the bride-to-be, in fact—went out onto the dance floor with a creature Steve recognized. A creature he had no respect for and would not let interfere with this particular group of women.

He had to act. Pushing away from the wall, Steve strolled onto the dance floor and positioned himself opposite Jorge, a Peruvian vampire who'd moved to the area recently. The bloodletter was already treading on thin ice with the local Master of his kind for preying a little too openly on humans. He hadn't killed anyone yet—that they knew of—but he'd been warned repeatedly to be more discrete in his feeding.

Steve made sure he caught Jorge's eye, and with a grudging sort of compliance, Jorge finished the dance and escorted the woman back to her friends. He left her with them and glanced over at Steve, cocking his head. Steve looked toward a quiet corner and Jorge nodded almost imperceptibly.

They both moved toward the corner. Steve stood for a

moment while the vampire did one of his magic tricks and dampened the sound so they could talk. It was amazing what some of the older vamps could do. They had a weird sort of magic all their own, very unlike anything Steve had seen human magic users do.

"Handy," Steve mused. "Thanks for the moment of quiet."

"You wanted to talk with me?" Jorge prompted, clearly annoyed, but Steve didn't give a shit.

The Redstone Clan was the most powerful group in this city, and even the Master knew it. This guy should show a little more respect, even if he was a few hundred years old. Steve could still crush him like an egg. And he wouldn't even need backup from his Clan to do it. Jorge just wasn't as tough as he apparently thought he was.

"I'd like you to leave those women alone." Steve didn't owe the vampire any more explanation than that, though he sensed Jorge was going to be difficult.

"Why should I? They are human, are they not?" Jorge looked over the small group who went on talking, laughing and drinking, unaware of the discussion in the corner.

"Yep. Human," Steve agreed. "And under my protection. Got it?" He leaned forward, doing his best to intimidate the shorter man.

"What's in it for me if I do you this favor?"

Steve had to stifle a sigh. This little twerp really didn't understand the gravity of the situation, and he certainly didn't know his place in the hierarchy around these parts. But Steve didn't want to be the heavy. It wasn't necessary and it would take too much time.

"I would be grateful. And I won't tell Tony you've been sniffing around the tourists again. I heard he warned you off...what was it? Three times, already? You should know better by now, Jorge."

Antoine de Latourette was the local Master vampire. His friends called him Tony. He was more than seven hundred years old and not someone to cross lightly.

Jorge finally got the message and straightened from his insolent slouch against the wall. He looked miffed, but Steve didn't care. It was time somebody taught this little pipsqueak a lesson.

"Instead of harassing me, maybe you ought to put a leash on some of your own." Jorge sneered as he looked pointedly over at the group of women.

Steve looked too.

"Shit." Things were getting more complicated by the moment. He turned back to Jorge. "Do we have an understanding?"

Jorge nodded, dropped the barrier he'd held that kept the blaring sound of the club at bay and turned to go without another word. It was disrespectful, but Steve didn't care at the moment. The group of seven women had been joined by a small Pack of wolves he knew well.

What was it with Derek's little sister that she—or her group of friends—were drawing out all the Others tonight? It couldn't be helped. Steve was going to find out for himself.

He set out across the crowded room just as a fight broke out. The violence quickly spread toward him, but he had his objective clear in mind. He wasn't going to let anything stop him from making it to the small group of women. He'd promised Derek he'd take care of his sister. Letting her get hurt in a bar fight was not going to happen on his watch.

Somebody threw a punch at Steve. He barely paused to return the favor, sending the stupid human flying several feet back, out of Steve's way. Another idiot tried to block his way with a barstool. Steve made short work of him but he started to wonder why seemingly disinterested bystanders were suddenly keen to stop him from getting to the women.

Steve whistled and one of the wolves perked up, looking through the crowd. Steve caught his eye and gave him a silent signal. *Guard. Protect.* Instantly, the stance of the young wolves went from merely protective of the women, which they'd been already, to on guard. *Good dogs,* Steve thought with a fleeting moment of humor as yet another human tried to block his path.

One of the wolves made as if to come help him, but Steve signaled him back. *Protect the women*, he sent via the hand signals everyone in the Redstone Clan knew. This group of wolves was part of one of the construction crews and they were mostly reputable. A little rough around the edges maybe, but good men all. Steve was sort of relieved to have them here now that the situation had taken an unexpected turn.

Steve paused momentarily to parry a few punches aimed his way but he didn't let the concerted attacks slow him down. He kept his eyes on the prize, making his way one opponent at a time, toward Trisha Morrow.

The club was great, but when the fight broke out on the other side of the packed dance floor, Trisha sobered enough to realize they probably should leave. Only there were a bunch of handsome men—big bruisers, most of them—flirting with the girls and none of her friends seemed sober enough to realize there might be danger if the fight kept escalating in their direction.

Trisha looked around and her gaze was caught by one man. A big, muscular man. He was as big as her brother, Deke, and just as good in a fight. He was walking toward her but kept getting waylaid by idiots who wanted to fight. Why they tried to hit *him*, she'd never know. Even she could see he wasn't interested in the melee. He was just trying to get from one side of the club to the other, and he didn't really seem to care who he had to mow down to do it.

There was something so elemental about the way he moved. Like a panther on the prowl. He vanquished one opponent after another—sometimes more than one at a time—sweeping them out of his way as if they were nothing. He sent a few guys sailing through the air. Some went down hard on the grimy floor. A few turned away when he growled at them.

He actually *growled*. She could hear the low rumble of it, even across the distance that still separated them. Why in the world did she find that sexy?

"Guys?" Trisha tried to get the attention of her drunk friends while her gaze remained on the warrior.

That's the only word she could think of to describe him. He had to be like Deke and most of the guys in her family. Military. Spec Ops. If not, then some kind of mercenary or professional killer.

That last thought almost made her giggle with nerves as their eyes met. And held.

Even as he threw two more would-be fighters aside, he kept his gaze on her. When he had to look away to throw a punch or block a barstool being thrown at him, it was only momentary. As soon as he'd dealt with the obstacle, he looked straight back at her again.

It was about that time she realized he wasn't just moving across the room. He was actually aiming for her table. For *her*.

Her foggy mind didn't understand the animal attraction that reared up and made her want to purr when she realized that hunk of dangerous manhood was making a beeline to her side. The rest of the raucous room faded to nothing as she watched his muscles bunch and flex as he dealt with one miscreant after another. *Yowza*. He was hot.

Hot and dangerous. The ultimate bad boy. *Mrawr*.

"The fighting is getting worse," she heard one of the men who'd come to chat with her friends say to the other over her head.

One part of her fuzzy mind wondered at their calm. The men had come to flirt and her girlfriends had happily obliged, but when the fighting started, the men had stayed with them, taking up what looked like guarding positions, now that she thought about it. She'd seen it often enough with the guys in her family in the past. It didn't take much to bring out the legendary Morrow protective streak. She'd dealt with it all her life.

Sometimes annoying, it was often nice to have a bunch of big, strong guys to watch your back and catch you if you fell. She'd relied on her dad and brothers for a lot of years to do just that. Though, to be honest, she hadn't needed rescuing in a long, long time.

"Steve said to stay here," the other man answered, still over her head as she watched the warrior get closer.

"Yeah, all right. But not for much longer. If he doesn't haul ass, we're going to have to start knocking some heads together. It'd be easier to just take the women outside, where it's safe," the first one said.

"You notice something funny about the fight? They're going after Steve," the second one observed. "It's subtle, but it's there. Could be, the ones who started the brawl *want* us to go outside. There's only four of us."

"Not for long," the first one replied. "I just called in the cavalry." Trisha heard a phone beep on her right side. The first guy had called someone and she could only hope he was on the right side of all this mayhem. Based on what she'd overheard, he probably was.

For whatever reason, a guy named Steve had told these guys to stay and watch over the girls. That didn't make much sense. She didn't remember any of the men being introduced as Steve. Had this Steve instigated the fight? It didn't sound that way, but the question remained… Who was Steve? And why would he tell these men—perfect strangers—to protect her small group of friends?

Unless…

Oh, no. He wouldn't have.

But she knew he would. Dammit. She could smell her brother's interference in this. He had friends all over the place, and she'd just bet one of his old Army buddies lived in Las Vegas. It didn't take much to imagine Deke calling ahead once she'd told him where the bachelorette party was being held.

Well. She could either get mad or be grateful that her big brother cared enough to get someone to keep an eye on them. In the normal course of business, she would have been pissed. But she was drunk and the fight was getting seriously out of control. Even she had to admit, she and her friends probably needed a knight in shining armor right now. Maybe a few of them.

Still, she knew she'd be mad at Deke later, when everything was sane again. When there were no flying beer bottles or bar stools, and no big men trying to beat the crap out of each other ten feet from where she stood.

"You guys know my brother?" she asked of the men at her side, proud when her words slurred only a little. She really shouldn't have had that row of test tube shots. She didn't even know what had been in them. But they were yummy.

"Sorry, doll. We don't know your brother," the guy on her left answered in a somewhat condescending tone.

"I don't like you," she blurted out, unable to filter her words in her drunken state. "Sorry," she apologized belatedly, but she heard laughter from both of the guys that flanked her.

"It's okay. He gets that reaction a lot," the guy on the right guffawed at his buddy's expense.

"So who's Steve?" She really wasn't very subtle when she was drunk.

"Heard that, did you? You mean you don't know him already?" The guy on the left seemed recovered from her insult and a little more respectful this time when he spoke to her.

"No. Should I?" She almost looked at them, but the man who'd been casually fighting his way to her was almost upon them. She couldn't tear her eyes away from him. He was even more good looking the closer he got.

"Yeah, judging by the way he just cleared a path to you, I kinda figured you two were already acquainted." The guy on the left turned as the fighting drew nearer. He was watching the crowd, but she only had eyes for the guy who stopped right in front of her.

"You're Steve," she stated. Darnit, she was drunk. She was just blurting out whatever came into her mind, no matter how inane.

The gorgeous warrior cocked his head to the side, clearly puzzled. "I am. And you're Trisha, right?"

She nodded, making herself dizzy in the process. "How do you know my name? We weren't introduced. I'd remember." He had the greatest smile. She was glad she was still leaning against the barstool because her knees were in serious danger of melting when he flashed that crooked smile at her. His eyes actually twinkled. And glowed.

Wait a minute. Glowed?

She must be even drunker than she thought. That round of test tubes was starting to roil in her stomach and slide right into her bloodstream. Things were getting blurrier, not better. What was *in* those things?

*Damn.* Steve smelled drugs. The chemical-metallic tang of something bad came off her in waves—and not much else. The chemical scent was so strong it was overpowering her normal female scent.

"Trisha, do you feel all right?" Steve hated this. She might've taken the drugs or she might've been slipped something. Right now, he didn't know which, and the fight was getting too damn close for comfort.

"No," she admitted in a wobbly voice as she leaned heavily on the bar stool.

Steve paused to push two of the fighters behind him farther back. So far, the small group of wolves had been keeping the fighting at bay around the drunk women, but he didn't know how much longer they could keep the status quo. Things seemed to be escalating instead of dying down.

And that didn't seem right either. Something strange was definitely in the air tonight.

"Steady now," he said in as soft a tone as he could manage over the loud noise of the fight. "Do you normally use drugs? Weed, crack, heroin?" He tried to be matter-of-fact about it, but he hated asking these questions.

"Piss off," she cussed him, making him want to smile. "I'm not a druggie. I'm just drunk."

"Do you *feel* just drunk, as you put it?" he challenged. He liked her spirit. She was feisty for a human.

She paused for a moment and her tongue peeped out to run over her lips. The sight of that little wet, pink muscle made his dick rise. *Shit.*

"Now that you mention it…" She paused to try to bring her hand to her face and missed. She was definitely not all right. Her coordination was shot. "Those test tube thingies must've been stronger than I thought," she finished lamely. "I'm higher than a kite." She smiled, then frowned. "I don't like it."

She made him want to laugh again, which surprised the hell out of him. She was kind of cute and very frank when she was out of it. It was an absurdly charming combination.

"I just got a text. The rest of the Pack is waiting for us outside," Jed Robinson reported from Trisha's right. He was the most senior of the wolves that had been flirting with Trisha and her friends. "There was some trouble out there, but they've neutralized it."

He understood what the wolf was trying to say. There'd been an ambush waiting for the women. But why? Steve didn't like this at all, and he didn't understand what it was about this group of women that had attracted all this attention, but he would. Before this night was over, he'd learn why they were such a target.

"All right, let's get out of here. The fight is more than the bouncers can handle and the cops will probably be here any moment. Unless you want to spend the rest of the night in jail, you should probably come with us, Trisha."

She looked at him again, giving him a good once over.

"You've got to be my brother's friend," she surprised him by stating. "If anyone here was his go-to guy, it would be someone like you. You've got the look. Okay." She paused, seeming to need to gather her wits. "I'll go with you. If you can convince me that you served with him."

How she knew her brother had called for backup in Vegas, he didn't have to guess. Deke was pretty protective of his family, but Steve respected that about the man. Now he just had to prove to his cautious sister that he was the inside man.

"Deke and I served in Afghanistan together." A few other places too, but those were classified. "My name is Steve Redstone."

"Shit," she cursed under her breath, but he heard it. "You're Red."

"At your service," he replied, knowing they really didn't have time to dally. The fight was really out of control and moving ever closer, though the wolves frowning presence kept most of it at bay. "Now can we get out of here?"

"Sure thing." She tried to stand but her legs clearly wouldn't support her. Still, she gave it her best shot until she managed to stand, leaning heavily on the small table.

She put one hand to her lips and issued an ear-splitting whistle. Her friends—most of whom were as drunk as she was, or worse—immediately looked at her. Well, that was one way to get the ladies' attention.

"This is my brother's friend Red," she shouted to her friends. "We're getting out of here."

Slow nods and a few worried looks answered her pronouncement, but the women did start moving. Purses were gathered. Short, tight skirts were pulled downward as they hopped off bar stools. Flirtatious hands sought the werewolves' arms for support, but all the women managed to stand, though several of them swayed alarmingly.

Steve put his hands out to catch Trisha as she almost fell over, but she managed to right herself and take a few steps before she nearly slid to the floor. Steve caught her on the way down and put one arm around her waist, holding her as she took wobbly steps toward the door. He would have carried her, but she was still able to walk and he wanted at least one arm free to fight, if need be.

"We took cabs here," Trisha babbled as they headed toward the door. She fit nicely against him.

"I know," he admitted, watching everything carefully.

The wolves were flanking the group of women, with Jed on point and Steve bringing up the rear. It was as good an arrangement as they could manage until they got outside. Luckily, the door wasn't that far away.

"I guess I shouldn't be surprised." She kept talking while they neared the exit. "How long have you been following me? Since I landed, I bet. Deke probably called you the moment we left home."

"Not quite. I only picked up your trail about two hours ago. Deke held off calling as long as he could, but the guy's always had a sixth sense for trouble. Guess he was right, eh?" Steve paused long enough to deliver a back kick to the guy about to attack them from the behind.

She gasped as the man went flying and didn't answer. Steve hustled her out the door and into the protection of the wolf Pack that was waiting outside. Jed was organizing the women into waiting vehicles. It was a measure of how far gone the women were that they didn't really question who the guys were or where they were going. It was more than obvious to Steve that they'd all been dosed with something that had not only altered their scents, but also decimated their better judgment.

The way to the three vehicles had been cleared and kept that way by the wolves. Steve tossed the keys to his Harley to one of the younger guys, knowing he'd follow on the motorcycle. Steve wasn't letting go of Trisha. She'd been drugged and nearly abducted. She wasn't leaving his sight until this was all sorted out.

He helped her into the back of the last vehicle, a big SUV driven by the wolf Pack's Alpha, Pete Newmar, whom Steve both liked and respected. Pete had been in the Marine Corps for a while. He'd left the Corps and learned his trade as a stone mason. In fact, he was one of the finest Redstone Construction employed and in charge of many of the really finicky projects that clients loved. He held rank not only within his own Pack of wolves, but within the larger Redstone Clan that encompassed everyone who worked for Redstone Construction—almost all of whom were shapeshifters of one kind or another.

The moment the doors were closed, Pete took off. One of the other girls was sitting next to Trisha, who was in the center of the back bench seat. Pete's youngest son, Jeremy, was in the front passenger seat.

Steve's sensitive hearing picked up the sound of his beloved Harley bringing up the rear. They made a neat little convoy as they headed out of the city and drove toward the development on the outskirts of Las Vegas where the Redstone Clan had settled.

Steve checked their back trail, as he knew the others were also doing. So far, there was no sign of pursuit.

"Where are you taking us?" Trisha's head lolled against the back of the seat, as did her friend's. The only difference between the two women was that Trisha was a little more awake.

"To safety," Steve was quick to assure her. "You can call Deke if you want to make sure we're on the level."

"Are you kidding?" She shot him a look full of disbelief. "I'd sooner paint myself green and stroll naked down Main Street. No, thank you." She was carefully enunciating each of her words and Steve guessed it took a lot of effort.

He admired her grit and he had to laugh at her reaction to calling her big brother. Steve would think long and hard before he made that call. On the one hand, Deke had always been a great man to have on his side in a fight. On the other, Deke probably wouldn't be all that rational when it came to his sister. And there was the paranormal aspect of all this to consider. As far as Steve knew, Deke had no idea there really were such things as werewolves, vampires and all the rest, much less that Steve himself was a werecougar.

"So we're going to your place?" Trisha insisted on picking up the thread of the conversation, such as it was. "Is it big enough for all of us?"

"We can take them to the Pack house," Pete volunteered from the front. "There's plenty of room there for all of them."

Steve realized that was probably the best plan. Wolf Packs

tended to enjoy the company of their Pack mates a lot more than other kinds of shifters, and they often built big Pack houses where the entire Pack could congregate for meals or events. It was also a rooming house, of sorts, designed to help out Pack members or friends in need. There were probably enough suites in the place this Pack had built to give every one of the women a place of their own.

"Sounds good," Steve agreed with Pete, then turned back to Trisha, who was now leaning against him. She was a nice, warm bundle at his side, and Steve was sorely tempted to put his arm back around her. "Trisha, I'm not sure how much of this you'll remember, but the man driving is my friend Pete. His son Jeremy is the one who helped your friend into the car. He's in the passenger seat. They have a bed and breakfast. That's where we're going. Okay?"

Steve tried to keep it simple and at the same time wanted to reassure her that she was in safe hands. She seemed calm, but that could be a byproduct of whatever drug she'd been given. He didn't want to cause her any more distress.

She nodded, then clutched her stomach and made a face that Steve understood all too well.

"You'd better pull over quick, Pete," Steve instructed, taking Trisha's free hand.

"The lead car just pulled over too," Pete reported as he rolled to a stop on the side of the desert road. "One of the gals is barfing into a cactus."

# CHAPTER TWO

Steve heard Pete's words from inside the SUV while he threw open the door and helped Trisha out. She stumbled, so he put his arm around her middle, holding her when she doubled over and emptied her guts into the shrubbery. It was hard to watch, but he knew she'd be better off getting the remnants of the toxic brew she'd been given out of her system as quickly as possible. This was one way. Humiliating, but expedient.

"Oh, God. I'm so sorry," she gasped between bouts of gagging and upchucking. "This is so embarrassing."

"It's okay. I've got you, Trish. Better out than in." Steve tried to soothe her.

He knew from past experience with his own sisters that most women really hated to be embarrassed. Steve held Trisha's hair back from her face for her and rubbed her back, trying to ease the tension that overtook her body every time she vomited the vile liquid that had very nearly poisoned her.

The chemical smell was even more overpowering now that it was out in the open, and Steve was glad whatever it was hadn't had time to get completely absorbed into her system. She was wobbly enough with the little she had already digested. He hated to think what would result from the full dose.

Pete got out of the SUV and rummaged around in the back for a moment. Reappearing at Steve's side, he held an open plastic bottle of wet wipes.

"Bebe had these in the back from our last picnic. They might help the lady," Pete said by way of explanation.

"Thanks." Steve took a wad of the wet wipes out of the bottle and nodded. "The other woman could probably use those too."

Pete sent Jeremy ahead with the bottle of wipes while Steve saw to Trisa. She was trembling in his arms, but the bouts of vomiting were coming to an end. He spread out one of the wipes and pressed it to her forehead. She sighed and reached up, taking it from his hand with shaking fingers. She wiped her face and mouth while Steve pressed another clean wipe to her forehead.

"Are you feeling any better?" he crooned, hating to see her in such distress.

"Shoot me now," she whispered and Steve had to chuckle at her response.

"Not gonna happen. You're too pretty to shoot," he teased.

She straightened from her bent-over posture and stood on shaky legs while Steve supported her. Her back was warm against his front and he marveled again at the nice way they fit together. It was rare he found a woman tall enough to fit him.

"Is my bag somewhere around here?" she asked, breaking into his dangerous thoughts. "There should be a bottle of water in it. I'd really like that, if you can find it."

"It's in the car. Can you walk or do you need my support?"

"I'm okay. I'd just really like the water." He noted that she'd sidestepped his question, but he let it go. She was standing on her own for now. Walking would come.

Steve got the big bag out of the back of the SUV and brought it back to her. No way was he going to rummage around in her purse without her permission and direction. He knew from growing up with his sisters that women's purses were sacred territory. Enter at your own peril.

"Unzip it," she directed as he fumbled with the big, slouchy leather bag. He held the opened bag up for her inspection, glad when she reached in and pulled out a bottle of water on the first try.

She uncapped the thing with trembling fingers and then took a sip, swishing and turning slightly to spit out the water into the scrubby grass at the roadside. It was obvious she was still embarrassed, but she was dealing with it. He liked that. In fact, the more he was around her, the more he liked *her*.

The water seemed to revive her as she was able to clean out her mouth and even swallow a sip. It was like watching a wilted flower revive before his eyes. Whatever had been in those cocktails she'd consumed had been potent, but now that a large portion of it was out of her system, she was starting to sober up.

She kept her back to him, walking a short distance away from the spot where she'd lost her dinner toward the other girl up ahead who was doing the same. Steve came up alongside her, sensing her concern for her friend.

"Lynda looks a lot worse than I was," she offered quietly.

Jed was supporting the other woman about twenty yards away as she continued to tremble. Even from this distance, the woman was surprisingly pale. Almost as if moonlight reflected off her skin. Trisha's friend Lynda was a stunner, he'd seen that from the moment he'd assessed the small group. But Steve had liked Trisha's earthier looks even better.

There was something about Trisha's long, dark hair and tall frame that had tempted him from fifty paces. Up close, she was even more gorgeous, while her friend was more elfin. Short, wispy, ethereal. Pretty, but not Steve's type. At least, not after he'd set eyes on Trisha.

"You're looking a lot better," Steve observed. "How are you feeling?"

She looked over at him and tried to smile. "Steadier all the time." She paused to dribble a little water onto a clean wet wipe he'd offered her. She ran the soft, wet square over her hands and arms. "This has to rank right up there with the most humiliating moments in my life. I apologize for…well…all of this. We just wanted to have one wild night out. Drink a little. Dance a lot. Somehow it all got out of hand."

"Nothing to be sorry for," Steve assured her. "Your brother has stood guard while I puked a few times more than I should admit to." He chuckled, remembering some of those early days in the service when he'd partied a little too hard.

"Oh, God. Deke. He's going to have conniptions when he hears about this." She took another wet wipe from Steve's hand and held it to her face. Her words were muffled when she spoke again. "Do we have to tell him?"

"I've been thinking about that. Trisha, you just said you and your friends intended to drink a little. Would you say you drank a lot more than you intended tonight? Or do you always down a row of shots all at once?"

The wipe came away from her face as she thought. Her expression was troubled. "I've never drunk that much in my life. I'd intended to have maybe one shot and a couple of mixed drinks over the course of the evening. That's usually my limit, but something…I don't really know what happened. The test tube things were so delicious."

"Do you know what was in them? Who ordered them?"

"I have no idea. They were just suddenly there and everyone was drinking them. I figured one of the girls must've asked for them, but it's kind of out of character for any of my friends to do that, now that I think about it."

"Damn. That's what I was afraid of." Steve reached for his cell phone.

"Who are you calling? Not Deke. Not yet." She looked a little upset with him, but Steve didn't let it stop him.

"No. Not Deke. Trisha, there's something going on here, and I have a buddy who specializes in finding stuff out. I'm calling him and his wife. She's a…nurse, of sorts. I want them both to get a look at you and your friends. Tonight.

Something bad happened here and I want to make sure you're all really okay."

In the moments it had taken him to speak, the call connected. Slade, the Clan's newest addition, answered on the second ring. Steve skipped the pleasantries, knowing the most magical shifter he knew had already seen the caller I.D.

"Can you and your lady meet me at Pete's Pack house? I'm bringing some civilians in with me who've been drugged. I don't think it was anything normal." Steve had to choose his words carefully in front of Trisha. He suspected something magical was happening here—and not the good kind of magic.

If that was the case, Slade and his new wife, Kate, who also served as the Clan's priestess, would be able to tell. Slade was also the best tracker this side of the Rio Grande, and he could be of some help if Steve had to do any hunting. Steve's inner cat stretched and growled, already eager to claw whoever had tried to harm Trisha.

"We'll be there in about fifteen minutes, barring more stops," Steve answered Slade's question about ETA. He was glad to hear Slade's response. He and the priestess would be there in twenty minutes. Good man.

Trisha walked toward her friend while Steve spoke to Slade and followed behind at a slower pace. She talked with the shaky woman for a few minutes, reassuring her that they were among friends and that Steve—or Red, as she called him—was a friend of her brother. The pixie-looking woman seemed uncertain, but when she looked directly at Steve, he saw her eyes flare.

The pixie was magical. Steve just knew it, even though he didn't have the gifts Slade had. Slade and his lady were actually able to actually *see* magic. Steve couldn't see it—not like they did—but he often sensed it when it was in the air. His spidey senses were tingling now, looking at the short beauty.

He'd seen that kind of unearthly elegance before. If he didn't miss his guess, that girl was at least part fey. He didn't understand why he hadn't seen it before. Although, to be honest, he'd been so preoccupied with Deke's sister, he'd only given a cursory look to her friends.

The evening began to make a little more sense. Jorge had probably been attracted by the scent of fey magic, even if he didn't realize exactly what it was. That kind of thing could easily make the pixie and all her friends targets of Others who weren't on the right side of the Light. Magic could be drained and used by evil and these girls were no match for some of the things Steve knew went bump in the night around these parts.

Steve found it interesting that of the seven women only these two had gotten sick so far. The others were sleeping it off in the backs of the vehicles. Steve could see them as he walked past the open doors.

He disconnected the call and met up with Trisha as she walked back toward him. She was looking a lot better. Better than her friend, in fact, as she sipped lightly from her water bottle. Steve had watched as she'd fished out another bottle of water from her voluminous bag and given it to her friend. The pixie-woman was going a little easier on actually drinking the water, but had used it to freshen up.

"Deke talked about you a lot, Red," she surprised him by saying as she walked beside him back to the SUV. "You and your brother, who Deke seems to think of as some sort of god among men."

Steve had to laugh at that description of his brother Grif, who was Alpha of one of the largest and most powerful Clans in the States. Despite all the shifter might at his command, Grif was a humble man. He'd been a fearless soldier and had served alongside Steve as an Army Green Beret. Grif had retired a bit before Steve. He was older and had to come back and take care of the Clan, but he'd earned a reputation among the younger men that Steve had benefited from as his brother.

Not that Steve hadn't earned his own rep. He'd enjoyed his time in the service. Sometimes he thought being a Spec

Ops soldier was the only thing he'd ever done in his life to really distinguish himself. He'd retired at a higher rank than his older brother, which was an accomplishment and something Grif didn't begrudge him. They had never really competed in that way. It was well established that they were both Alphas in their own right, but that Grif was the Alpha in charge of the entire Clan.

Steve was his right-hand man, in charge of security for the immense group of various kinds of shifters that formed the Redstone Clan. Steve also held the official position of Chief Security Officer in the family company. Redstone Construction was one of the largest and most successful building firms in the country.

"Grif's just a regular guy," Steve replied to her veiled inquiry. "You'll see that when you meet him." He was, of course, much more than a man, but unless she was playing dumb a lot better than he gave her credit for, Trisha didn't seem aware of the real, *magical* world hidden all around her.

"You mean he lives around here? I hope I have time to clean up first before I meet the living legend." Steve liked her sense of humor. She was speaking in jest and he had to smile at her words.

"We're a pretty close-knit family. I have four brothers, all of whom ostensibly live in Las Vegas, though two of them tend to travel more than the rest of us. The youngest, Matt, likes to spend time in California, and the one right below me in age, Mag, is off to parts unknown lately. But Bob's here, as is Grif. You'll probably meet them both within the next few hours or days—depending on what we find out about the bar fight tonight and how well your friends recover from whatever you were all drugged with."

She stopped short. "So you think we really were slipped something?" She seemed to get clearer as time went on, recovering well after her bout with the poisonous substance that had been fed to her.

"I have little doubt. You look a lot better now. How are you feeling?" He held the door for her as they arrived back at the SUV.

"Like a fog is slowly lifting and I'm finally able to start thinking again." She paused by the door, her eyes scrunching up as she seemed to ponder her words. "Darnit. That stuff was strong, whatever it was." She reached out and took the last of the clean wet wipes from Steve's hand before getting into the SUV and sliding over on the bench seat.

Steve got in after casting his eye over the rest of the little convoy. Everyone was accounted for and nobody was on the scrubby desert road except them. The motorcycle was heading back toward them after checking their back trail and the pattern he blinked on his headlight signaled that all was clear as far as he could see.

So far, so good. Now all he had to do was get them the rest of the way to the Pack house without further incident.

Steve shut the door and the convoy took off once more. He shouldn't have been surprised to see Trisha wiping the face of her friend with the last of the wet wipes. Trisha took her friend's pulse in a very professional way and looked her over, including peeking under her eyelids to check her eyes.

"She's really out cold," Trisha reported as she turned around and sat facing forward once more. "But her breathing is steady and her pulse is good. I think she'll be okay, but I can't tell much without my go bag."

"You have a go bag?" Steve was surprised, but then he really didn't know what Trisha did with her life besides being Deke's sister and the apple of his eye.

Trisha rested her head against the back of the seat and closed her eyes briefly. "I'm a doctor. A researcher, really. I don't deal with patients much. Mostly I work in a lab, behind the scenes, playing with Petri dishes and cellular solutions."

Steve was impressed. Not only was she gorgeous, but brainy too.

The SUV rounded a corner and Trisha turned to her friend, who lolled towards her, completely unconscious. Trisha settled her friend again and turned back toward Steve, her lower lip caught between her teeth as she chewed on it in worry.

Steve tried hard not to look at her mouth. Looking at her mouth only brought uncomfortable thoughts to mind. Thoughts about what he'd like to do to that mouth—and what he'd like that mouth to do to him.

"I wish I knew what we'd been dosed with. Darnit! I should've taken samples back there." She looked at Steve, clearly thinking fast. "Do you know where I could find a lab nearby? Maybe there's a hospital or testing facility I could talk my way into?"

"It's not a medical facility, but Redstone Construction has a quality control lab with all the latest equipment."

"Redstone Construction? That's you? I mean, Deke calls you Red because your last name is Redstone, right?" She shook her head. "I'm not making sense. Sorry." She smiled at him and he felt his lips twitch in response. "Do you mean to tell me you're one of *those* Redstones?"

"Yes, ma'am. Second eldest and head of security for Redstone Construction. If you want to see if our lab suits your needs, I can give you full access."

"Wow. Even I have heard of your family's company. They just finished building the new children's wing on the hospital back home. It's gorgeous. All state of the art, and I have friends on the hospital board. You guys didn't overcharge."

"We're in this business for the long haul," Steve repeated what he'd often heard his older brother and even their father say. "We don't cut corners and we don't work solely for profit. There's satisfaction in a job well done and all our people feel that way."

"It shows. I've seen a few of the bigger projects your company has completed." She nodded, visibly weary, but her mind appeared to be racing even as she leaned her head back against the seat. "So that extends to having your own QC lab, huh? I'd like to see it. If nothing else, I might be able to isolate the compound from a blood sample. I'd need a centrifuge, but most labs have those. And I could jury rig a column from some glassware. It'll depend what kind of

machinery you have as to how I can identify the compound."
She yawned, though she kept talking. "Do you know if you
have anything like a mass spectrometer or infrared
spectrograph? Maybe a gas chromatograph?"

"We have all those," he confirmed, glad he'd kept up his
interest in chemistry and the lab their mother had founded
and kept current until her recent, untimely death.

"Really?" She looked over at him, her head remaining on
the back of the chair as fatigue seemed to creep up on her
again. "You guys must take quality control very seriously."

Steve shrugged. "It was a pet project of my mother's
before she passed on. She liked to tinker."

He didn't mention the advanced degree in molecular
chemistry that his mother had pursued later in her life. She
had always been a fearless woman who would try anything,
even as she served as Matriarch to one of the largest Clans in
North America. She'd had a heart as big as the world and
curiosity to match. Nothing had stopped her pursuit of
learning and of helping shifters in need. Humans too, if they
crossed her path.

Steve felt a little pang and knew his mother was in a better
place, but it still hurt that she'd been taken from this earth
too soon. Murdered by magic, she hadn't stood a chance, and
the family had gone a little nuts for a while. But Slade had
come and helped find the killer…and then he'd stayed and
married the new priestess. He'd become a good friend and a
tremendous help as the Redstone family and Clan tried to
carry on and heal from the staggering loss.

Thankfully, the small convoy arrived at the Pack house at
that moment and he didn't have to talk more on the painful
subject. Steve took a quick look around and waited for the all
clear from the lead vehicle before getting out. He helped
Trisha stand and supervised while her friend was picked up
and carried into the welcoming light of the big wooden and
adobe structure.

Several of the werewolf Pack's women were there,
including Pete's wife, Bebe, the Alpha bitch of the Pack. She

was organizing where each of the unconscious women were taken. They were given a set of seven rooms, all on the second floor of the house along the same corridor.

Trisha went ahead to walk with her friend Lynda—the only other woman who was still conscious. They oversaw the comfort of their friends as one by one, they were delivered to small bedrooms. The werewolf women helped make each of the unconscious human women comfortable while Trisha and Lynda clucked over their fallen friends and looked worried.

Steve stood back, watching to see what he could do to help when Pete joined him. "We weren't followed," he reported. "At least not that our guys can see. And your brother called. He's coming over with Slade and the priestess."

Bebe came down the hall, joining them at the point where the long hall joined the upstairs landing of a wide staircase. She was frowning and wringing her hands—something very uncharacteristic for the Alpha female. Steve went on alert.

"They don't smell right," Bebe reported the moment she joined them.

"They were dosed with some kind of drug—" Steve began, but she cut him off.

"More than that. There's the scent of magic in it too. Bad magic."

Steve frowned. He knew Bebe had a tiny bit of mage in her bloodlines way back somewhere, though she was a fully capable shapeshifting werewolf. Still, she had a sense about magic that most shapeshifters didn't. If she said she smelled magic on the women, he believed her.

"Okay. Let's limit the exposure of our people, just in case. I'd advise you to call your women back and keep them occupied elsewhere until we have this figured out. Alpha, I'd recommend the same for your guys." Steve was careful to respect the wolves' right to rule in their own Pack house.

Besides, both Pete and Bebe were older than him by about a hundred years. They'd helped raise him and had been close friends of his parents, when they'd been alive. A certain amount of respect came second nature when dealing with the older Alpha couple.

"Agreed," Pete responded thoughtfully. "We'll keep everyone out of this corridor. There are three more rooms here that are unoccupied right now. We'll keep those empty and limit the humans to this area unless they have escort. At least five of them won't be moving around much for now. The other two…" Pete nodded at something down the hall and Steve realized Trisha and Lynda were walking toward them, arm in arm as they moved slowly down the long hall.

"Trisha is my responsibility," Steve said at once in a low, urgent voice. "Her brother is a good friend of mine and he asked me to keep an eye on her while she was in town."

"What about the fey?" Bebe asked as they watched Lynda leave Trisha at the door to one of the closer rooms. Trisha disappeared inside and then the stunning pixie squared her shoulders and headed directly for them.

"Looks like we're about to find out," Steve muttered.

Lynda stopped before the *were* trio and bowed her head, though she didn't break eye contact.

"Thank you for coming to our rescue tonight. I know what you are, though I'm not entirely sure *who* you are. Trisha says you're her brother's Army buddy?" The surprising woman looked directly at Steve.

"I am. Her brother called and asked me to keep an eye on her and your group while you were in town."

The pixie looked weary. "After what happened tonight, I'm really glad he did. And I thank you for interceding and bringing us to safety. I'm Lyndelia van Esperingan, but the humans know me as Lynda. They don't know what I am."

"Forgive me, but other than fey, what exactly are you?"

The pixie laughed quietly and the sound was almost enchanting. "Sorry. I'm only half-fey. My mother was a human mage. My father is a warrior prince currently living in another realm. I'm making a go of it here, but lately it's been one thing after another with lesser mages trying to trap me and steal my magic. Usually, I'm a lot better at defense than I have shown myself to be here in your territory. I'm very sorry. I wouldn't have come on the trip and endangered my human friends had I realized any of this would happen."

"So you believe they were after you?" Pete asked as Steve held off, watching and weighing the pixie's words.

"Whoever *they* are." She shrugged. "I've been hunted off and on for a few decades. There's been a slight uptick in the number of incidents just lately, but I didn't think anything could get past my defenses. I've learned my lesson after tonight." She made a face. "I would appreciate it if you didn't reveal my differences to my friends. I like being human and living among them as much as I can. I wouldn't want that to change because of tonight's misadventure."

On one level, Steve couldn't believe how selfish this woman sounded. On another, he sort of understood her desire to be just a normal human with no worries other than the normal human worries. But this little fairy was in for a rude awakening and Steve was just the man to deliver it.

"I won't reveal your secret, but you'd better wake up and realize the *Venifucus* are out there and they're gunning for every being who serves the Light. Even one as self-centered as you."

The pixie recoiled from Steve's accusation and he was glad she appeared to be thinking about his harsh words. Steve was building up a good head of steam when Pete put one hand on his arm, the gesture saying without words that Steve should be more cautious. He didn't like it, but this was Pete's territory. Steve needed to defer to the Alpha werewolf in his Pack house.

"We will not out you to the humans, but neither can we allow you to put either them or us in even more danger than we are already in. This Clan has already paid a terrible price to the evil of the *Venifucus* recently, and we have still not recovered from it."

"I don't understand." To her credit, the pixie-woman actually looked both confused and concerned. "The *Venifucus*. They don't exist. My father said they were vanquished

RED

centuries ago."

"How old are you, child," Bebe asked in a soft, motherly tone.

"I just turned seventy," Lynda answered in a small voice, clearly responding to Bebe's warmth.

"Och, you're just a baby by your people's standards. Ours too, come to think of it. You don't know much about the ancient troubles with the *Venifucus*, do you? And if you've been living completely among humans, you probably haven't heard the news that they are most definitely back. Come now, let's get you cleaned up and then we can have a long talk. I'll catch you up on everything that's been happening in the magical world while you've been playing at being human." Bebe put her arm around the much shorter woman's shoulders and led her down the hall, shooting a look back at the men that said *let me take care of this*, in no uncertain terms.

"Thank the Mother of All for Bebe," Pete muttered, and Steve had to agree.

"Do you have any blood-drawing equipment? Syringes, tubes, sterile pads. That kind of thing." Steve turned to Pete, already on to the next thing on his mental list.

"Sure, why?" Pete looked interested, and Steve was glad to explain. The Alpha would need to know what was going on in his Pack territory, especially right in the Pack house.

"Trisha is a doctor. She wants to try to identify the substance they were all dosed with. I said I'd take her by the lab and she seems eager to try to do something to help her friends."

"Won't they just sleep it off?" Pete frowned.

"Probably," Steve agreed. "But I can see her point in wanting to know exactly what it was they were given, in case there are any longer-lasting effects."

Pete nodded. "Hall closet should have what you need. I'm going downstairs to talk to everyone and meet Grif, Slade and Kate. I'll send them up when they get here."

"Thanks." Steve shook the older man's hand with genuine affection. Pete was like an uncle to him and always had been.

29

The men went their separate ways and Steve headed to the closet to gather supplies. His hands were full when he scented...something. Something stirring. Something amazing. Something...

He turned around, clutching the supplies to his chest as he stared down the hallway that led to where the human women were being housed for the time being. The alluring scent wafted nearer and he stood, transfixed as a terrycloth-covered female shape stepped into view. She was rubbing at her long, dark, wet hair and her face was obscured, but Steve knew exactly who she was.

She was his mate.

Now that the overpowering chemical smell had been scrubbed away from her body, Trisha's natural scent bombarded Steve's senses with an undeniable truth. She was his. The cat inside him stood up and yowled while the man stood, unable to move, frozen by the startling realization that lightning had finally struck.

Trisha Morrow was almost certainly his destined mate.

And her brother was going to kill him.

# CHAPTER THREE

"Oh, good. You found some supplies for me. Thanks." Trisha walked right up to him clothed only in a fluffy, white terrycloth robe and a towel draped around her neck to absorb the water still dripping intermittently from her hair. She wasn't shy about taking things out of his hands, her delicate fingers brushing against the fabric that covered his chest, heightening the instant arousal that had attacked him the moment he'd caught her true scent.

She seemed preoccupied by the crinkly wrapped syringes, alcohol wipes and various other first aid supplies he'd collected from the closet. She emptied his hands and turned to go, and he was powerless to do anything but follow in her wake. He was struck nearly dumb by the idea that he'd finally met his mate.

And she didn't know the first thing about the real world. She was human. Innocent of the knowledge that they were not the only highly advanced creatures that inhabited the earth. Even though she was friends with a half-fey, it was clear the pixie-woman—as Steve had come to think of her—was keeping her friends in the dark about Others.

Trisha didn't know. And her brother was one of his best friends in the human world. He didn't know either, though he often questioned some of the things he'd seen Steve do in the field that a regular human man wouldn't have been able to accomplish—even someone as skilled as Deke Morrow.

Deke was gonna murder him. There was no way around it.

"I'm going to take blood samples from everyone and then I'd like to go see your lab."

"What about sleep?" He had to object. It was for her own good.

He felt a new responsibility for her welfare—even above and beyond what he'd felt before knowing she was dear to a good friend of his. Suddenly, she'd become dear to *him*, personally, and he felt some kind of weird biological imperative to protect her in all ways.

"Oh, I feel fine now. The shower revived me." She peered back over her shoulder as he followed her down the hallway. "I'm good to go for a few hours yet. And I'd like to narrow down what's affecting my friends as soon as possible, just in case it's something worse than it appears."

"Maybe I can help with that," a new voice sounded from behind Steve. It was a mark of his preoccupation that he hadn't heard the priestess come up behind him.

He turned and made way for Kate, the priestess for the Clan, to pass.

"Hi, I'm Kate. I came to help." She held out her hand and took some of the nearly overflowing supplies out of Trisha's hands. "My husband, Slade, is the big guy creeping up on Steve."

*Dammit!*

Steve turned around and sure enough, there was Slade, one dark brow quirked in surprise. Then his icy-grey eyes turned to Trisha and back again, widening.

Slade slapped Steve on the back and grinned as he came even with him. "Your brother is downstairs talking things over with Pete. The others are on standby in case we need them. What do you think?"

Steve grimaced. Where the protection of his mate was concerned, there really was no alternative.

"We need them," he confirmed with a suppressed growl.

While he wanted to be near Trisha, Steve knew he needed some distance to get a grip on his reactions. Two people had just gotten the drop on him. Slade could almost be forgiven. The man shared his soul with the most magical of cat shifters and had spent most of his life as a covert operative. He had serious skills.

But Kate had no stealth skills to speak of. The fact that she'd walked openly up to him and he hadn't registered her presence told Steve he was dangerously off his game. Better to go away for a few minutes and regroup. He had to see his brother anyway and he trusted Slade to keep an eye on things up here for the moment.

"I'll go talk to Grif." Steve watched the two women enter one of the rooms, already chatting like old friends. "One of the women is half-fey. She's hiding it. The rest of them probably don't have a clue," Steve warned Slade as he turned to go.

"And the one with my mate?" Slade delayed him by asking.

"My friend's sister. The one I was asked to keep an eye on."

Slade frowned. "That makes it more complicated," he said cryptically. "I take it your friend doesn't know about us."

"He probably suspects. He saw a lot while we were deployed, but he's never come straight out and asked," Steve admitted.

"He's going to try to kick your ass when he finds out you're sweet on his sister," Slade observed as if it was obvious Steve had a thing for Trisha. Maybe it was. Slade could literally *see* magic. Maybe the bond between mates was something visible to him.

"Yeah, I know." Steve ran a hand over his short hair in frustration. "But there's nothing I can do about it. She's—"

"Your mate." Slade's tone was knowing, unambiguous.

Steve wanted to curse, but he also wanted to crow. After all these years, there *was* a woman for him. He'd given up hope. He'd made his life about his family and his Clan. He'd never expected to add a mate to that equation, but it looked like the Mother of All had other plans for him. Only he had no idea how it was going to work.

"She's human." He spoke his thoughts aloud.

Slade was silent for a long time. So long, that Steve looked over at the other man.

"What? You sense something about her?"

Slade's icy blue eyes narrowed at the spot down the hall where the women had gone. "Could be. Go talk to your brother. I'll check on my mate—and yours—and I'll let you know what I find out."

With those cryptic words, Slade prowled down the hall on silent feet. He shared his soul with two separate creatures—a black leopard and a Himalayan snowcat that came out to play only rarely because its appearance caused such a ruckus. Snowcats were considered holy beings among most other kinds of shifters, and Slade had a lot more magic than most. For one thing, he didn't have to disrobe in order to shift shape. That was a talent reserved for the most magical of creatures.

But Slade had also been—and still was, Steve privately thought—a highly placed covert operative for the Company. Steve didn't think Slade was still interested in going on missions, but Steve had little doubt the man kept his hand in. He had an information network that was as far reaching as it was well informed.

Steve stopped delaying and hustled down the stairs to see Grif. No doubt the Clan Alpha would have a few things to say about the guests his brother had brought home tonight. Steve wasn't looking forward to explaining any of this because he was as confused as he'd ever been. He'd have preferred a little alone time to think things through, but there was no help for it. Grif was here. It was time to face the music, even if he wasn't prepared to dance.

Grif stopped speaking mid-sentence when Steve walked into the front parlor of the Pack house. Not a good sign. The tension in the room escalated to a peak level and some of the younger and lower-ranked wolves started to fidget. The Clan Alpha wasn't pleased.

"We'll finish this in a few minutes. For now, lay low and avoid the humans as much as possible until we figure this all out," Grif told the gathered wolves.

It looked like all the folks currently living or serving at the Pack house and the two werewolf Alphas had been gathered into the room. With a nod from Grif, all the wolves but the Alphas got up and left on quiet feet, passing Steve with nervous smiles as they made their way out the door. When the last was gone, Steve closed the door and moved farther into the room.

"What were you thinking bringing them here, Steve?" Grif asked, clearly exasperated.

"Grif—" Steve tried to get a word in edgewise, but his older brother was clearly working up a good head of steam.

"With all the trouble we've had lately, you bring not one but *seven* complete strangers into the heart of our territory. And one of them is fey!" Grif cursed not completely under his breath. "Those damn fey bastards. You never know what side they're on."

"I didn't know about the fey girl until later," Steve admitted, knowing he wasn't helping his own case, but it was the simple truth.

"That's even worse. Dammit, Steve! You know better than this." Grif ran a hand through his hair in an impatient gesture. He'd let his golden locks grow pretty long since leaving the service, unlike Steve, who kept his military short. "I heard one of them is a friend's sister. Which one?"

"Do you remember Derek Morrow?"

"Deke? Shit. He asked you to keep an eye on his baby sister? He must trust you more than I realized. That guy used to go ape shit if anyone even mentioned his sister. Have you called him?"

"And have him and whoever he can scramble storm our territory with murder on his mind?" Steve laid out what they both knew would happen if he called Deke and told him his baby sister had been roofied. "No, thanks. And it just got more complicated."

"How could this get any more complicated?" Grif wanted to know.

"She took a shower." Steve didn't know how to say this, so he edged around it as best he could.

"Fuck man, you didn't jump her in the shower did you? No way you had enough time for that."

"Give me a little credit," Steve scoffed. Though if he was honest, if he'd known she was in the shower, he might've been tempted. "The problem is, the chemical scent washed off. And then I got a good whiff of her real scent. Bro, she's..." He didn't know how to say it.

"Oh, no. What?" Grif's eyes narrowed.

Steve sank to the couch and put his head in his hands. "She's my mate."

He had whispered his confession, but he knew the three Alphas in the room—Grif and the werewolf couple—heard him.

Silence greeted his words and Steve felt every moment of it. Finally, he couldn't stand it anymore and looked up to see the strangest expression on his older brother's face. It was a mix of happiness and concern. Steve understood that reaction all too well. He stood, moving restlessly.

"Deke is gonna serve your balls on a platter," Grif said finally, whistling between his teeth.

"Surely not," Bebe scoffed, coming closer. "Congratulations, Stevie. I'm so happy for you." She put her arms around him and pulled him downward so she could place a motherly kiss on his cheek and give him a squeeze. Steve let the diminutive form of his name roll over him. Nobody had called him that in a long time. Nobody but those who'd had a hand in raising him would dare. Bebe was one of the few. She was like an aunt to him and he felt a small pang for what his mother's reaction would have been had she still been around to offer her love and advice at this pivotal moment in his life.

"Congratulations, lad," Pete offered, shaking Steve's hand once Bebe let him go. "Does your lady know? Does she realize what it all means?"

And there was the crux of the problem. Steve had to shake his head in dismay. "She's human. She doesn't know about our world and I don't think she has any feelings for me one way or the other. If anything, she's either embarrassed that I saw her in a vulnerable moment or grateful that I was there to help her out. I have no idea if she's even attracted to me."

"You're a hunk," Bebe said with smiling confidence. "Of course she's attracted to you. And even better, she's your mate. If she doesn't realize it yet, don't worry, she'll come around."

"I wish I had your confidence," Steve admitted. "Trisha's human, Bebe. She probably doesn't feel the mating bond the way we do."

"She's more than that, actually." Slade's voice came to them from the open doorway.

Steve had been so caught up in his own problems that he hadn't really registered the slight click as the door opened. He was losing his edge and it was all because of the startling developments with Trisha.

"Sit rep?" Grif prompted Slade for the situation report as he came into the room and shut the door behind himself.

"She's magical. Very magical. In a way I've never really seen before. I think maybe she's got some nymph in her ancestry somewhere, but I can't be sure," Slade reported. "Kate's with her, helping her check on her friends and observing. I don't think she's dangerous to us, and she seems completely unaware of her nature—or at least unaware of the magical aura around her."

"You're kidding." Steve was surprised, to say the least.

"Certain kinds of nymphs are known for attracting the opposite sex. Is it possible she's not really Steve's mate?" Grif asked sharply.

"Good question," Slade said thoughtfully as all eyes turned

to Steve.

"Look…" Grif paused and sat down on the edge of the couch, defusing a lot of the tension in the room. His motions invited everyone else to do the same. "Let's start at the beginning. Tell me exactly what happened tonight and don't leave anything out."

Steve couldn't sit. He paced while everyone else listened to his recital of what had taken place that night. He started with the covert surveillance on the bachelorette party group. He'd picked up their trail from their hotel and followed them down the strip to the club where they'd been drinking steadily.

"They started out calmly enough. A few mixed drinks, a lot of laughter and jokes. I kept to the wall, far enough away that I couldn't smell them, but close enough to see what went down at their table." Steve ran a hand over the inch-long fuzz of hair he kept on top of his head. "After about twenty minutes, they started to attract the wrong sort of attention. Jorge, the new vamp in town, slithered in. I caught his attention and warned him off, but while I was having a little talk with him in the corner, the wolf pups moved in. Sometime during all this, the alcohol consumption had increased five-fold, at least. The girls suddenly had rows of test tube shots lined up. Each of them had a rack of the things. The tubes looked colorful and festive. Just like something a bunch of girls would order. I didn't think much of it except to realize that they'd probably be really drunk, very soon."

"So the pups moved in on the girls independently?" Pete wanted to know. "They had no idea you were watching that group, right?"

"That's the way it looked to me. They seemed surprised to see me when I left Jorge and moved toward them. About that time, a fight broke out, delaying me. When I finally got to the girls, I realized something was seriously wrong with those shots. The chemical scent was overpowering and their reactions were way over the top. I signaled one of yours…" Steve nodded toward the werewolf Alphas, "… and they called in the cavalry. They met us outside, where they'd foiled an ambush that was waiting by the door. My guess is that the fight was started to delay me and force the women out of the bar, where the trap would have been sprung."

"Somebody was targeting them," Bebe surmised with a frown. "Maybe the fey was attracting the wrong sort of attention? Or maybe your mate's magic attracted it, Stevie. I hate to say it, but we all know firsthand that there are evil folk out there who would easily prey upon such easy targets."

"Because there were so many wolves involved, it seemed right to bring the ladies here when you suggested it, Pete," Steve addressed the wolf Alpha with respect. "I'm sorry I've brought trouble to your door. I just didn't see any alternative. Yours is one of the few places equipped to take in so many strays. I'll reimburse you for whatever costs they incur and I'll reinforce your security with the Clan's, if you'll allow it."

"Done and done," Pete agreed with a serious nod. "And I understand why you brought them. I don't really blame you for it. Sometimes things just work out the way they work out." The older man shook his head.

"I wouldn't be surprised if it was supposed to work out this way," his wife agreed. "We'll help however we can, Steve. The security of your mate is important to all of us. We want to see you both happy and safe."

A little pang went through Steve's heart at the love Bebe displayed so casually in her words and her attitude. He missed his mother. She'd been ripped from his life by violence only a short while ago. He hadn't really healed from the loss yet. He'd moved on with his life, but there was a gaping hole where his mother used to be in his heart.

Bebe reminded him of that endless, boundless, unconditional, maternal love. She reminded him of his mother. His greatest champion no matter how old he got. His mother had understood him and counseled him and filled the role of wise elder for not only him, but the entire Clan. She was sorely missed.

"If she really is his mate," Grif reminded them.

In his heart, Steve had no doubts. His inner cat knew its mate. It wouldn't be fooled by nymph magic. It knew its heart's desire. And so did Steve. Even though it was going to cause problems for him with one of his best friends, Steve knew Trisha was meant to be his.

The question was, did she realize it? And if she didn't now, would she ever? She wasn't a shifter. She didn't have the same mating imperative wired into her DNA. Would she leave him and sentence him to a miserable life alone?

The sad truth was, he thought just maybe, she would.

She wouldn't mean to hurt him, but she didn't understand what mating among *weres* was all about. Hell, at this point, she didn't even know he *was* a shifter.

And to top it all off, she was probably still in danger from whatever or whomever had targeted her little group of friends. Once something evil got the scent of unprotected, naïve magic, it didn't easily let it go.

Whether it was the fey or Trisha herself that had attracted the evil, he didn't know. He didn't think it really mattered at this point, because all seven women—the humans too—were clearly in the crosshairs.

"Regardless, we must protect them all," Slade put in. "Kate's still upstairs with them, but I had a chance to talk over a few things with her. All of them will require a few days recuperation. They're not going to come out of the stupor any time soon. It's a magical as well as a mundane drug they've been given. The two who got sick—your woman, Steve, and the half-fey girl—reacted to some ingredient in the potion. Kate thinks it might've been silver, but she hasn't told Trisha that. Better to let her go to the lab and find out for herself. She's very intent on analyzing the substance they've been drugged with, so I suggest you take her to the lab at your earliest opportunity. She'll find out what happened on the physiological level while Kate and I will try to figure out what's going on magically. The half-fey woman agreed to help us there. Better to get Trisha out of the way for now. Let her do her doctor thing. Then figure out what we need to tell her as it comes." Slade sighed and ran one hand through his shoulder-length black hair. "If she really is your mate, Steve, we'll have to let her in on our secrets. If it's the drug—or her magic—then maybe we can skate."

Steve saw red but reined in his temper. "While I understand your caution, she *is* my mate, no matter what you think. I'll deal with her and I'll thank you all—" he paused to look around the room and eyeball each person in it, "—to leave her to me. She is my business. Not yours."

Everybody looked at Grif, wondering how the Clan leader would handle Steve's ultimatum. Slade bristled, as did Pete, but they both deferred to Grif, as it should be. Grif's jaw clenched visibly a few times before he spoke, a sign Steve recognized as his older brother's attempt to manage his own anger. Too bad. Steve wasn't backing down. Not about Trisha.

"If she poses a threat to the Clan, the wolf Pack or any of our people, she becomes our business, Steve. For now, I'll leave her to you. *For now,*" Grif repeated, emphasizing his words and his forbearance.

Fine. Steve would take that and run with it. He nodded toward his brother and headed for the door. He wanted to be with his mate. The cat wouldn't put off seeing her, basking in her scent, for another minute.

# CHAPTER FOUR

The lab Steve took her to wasn't far. It was housed in the corporate offices of Redstone Construction, which contrary to popular belief was housed in a two-story structure—nothing higher than a shifter could safely jump from—that resembled a house more than an office building. It was on the outskirts of the city on a wide parcel of land owned outright by the Redstone family.

"You said this was your mother's hobby?" Trisha ran her hand along the gleaming bench top as she walked farther into the big room. Everything was crisp and clean, the way Steve's mother had left it. "She must have been some hobbyist. I couldn't have asked for better in a laboratory that wasn't built expressly for medical purposes."

"Mom was a researcher, like you, only in chemistry, not medicine," he admitted, missing seeing his mother tooling around in here. "Although, she did like to tinker with plant genetics on occasion. Some of her work with drought-resistant plants was patented. It became an interest of hers when we moved to the desert."

"She sounds like a remarkable woman." Trisha turned to him, halting in front of the centrifuge.

"She was," he agreed in a quiet voice. Sometimes it was hard to hide the pain he still felt at her loss.

Trisha reached out to him and placed one soft hand on his arm. Tingles ran from where she touched him, all through his nervous system. His body definitely recognized the touch of its mate.

"Her death was recent, right? Deke told me he hadn't been able to make the funeral. He felt really bad about that. He wanted to be here for you."

"It's okay. The arrangements happened very quickly. She passed a couple of months ago. It was sudden. And violent. She was murdered."

"I'm so sorry. I hope they caught whoever was responsible."

"Yeah, we got them. In fact, Slade and Kate were instrumental in the hunt." Better to get her used to the idea that the Clan handled things on its own, rather than involve human authorities, a little at a time.

"Really?" She seemed both surprised and intrigued. "I thought they both worked for your construction firm."

"No, not at all, in fact. Slade only moved here recently when he married Kate. They met when he came to help track my mother's killer. He's got special skills in that area, and once he met Kate, well, it was clear they were meant to be together. He moved here to be with her since she's an integral part of our community."

As they talked, he helped her unpack the small cooler full of samples they'd brought with them from the Pack house. Trisha started to look through the drawers for the supplies she'd need and she smiled when she found the centrifuge tubes and pipettes. The smile of discovery was familiar to Steve. He'd pottered around in the lab with his mom often enough that he remembered the way she had smiled when she discovered something that helped her research.

That wasn't to say that Trisha reminded him of his mother. Not in the least. Well...a little. Maybe. In her quest for knowledge and her caring heart. In all other ways, she was unique. And uniquely fitted to him.

He started to think about a future spent by her side and he

liked the idea very much. It fit well with what he hoped for his future. A smart, caring mate. A happy life. All those things everyone sought in this world and seldom found.

Steve hadn't been sure he ever would find the woman meant for him. Having seen what he'd seen of the world and done all the things he'd done, he wasn't sure he really believed in happy ever after anymore. Until now. Until Trisha and her wonderful, alluring, amazing scent.

Maybe, just maybe, there would be a happy ending for him. If he could get her to agree to be his.

Not being a shifter, he didn't know how she would handle everything. It bothered him that she probably wouldn't feel the mating imperative the way he did. The fact that she didn't know about his people or his ability to become the cat that lived inside his soul was yet another thing to worry about. How could he tell her, only to have her reject him?

Right now, that was his biggest fear. He didn't think he could live through her rejection. For one of the very rare times in his life, Steve was truly afraid.

"What does Kate do? I thought she was the company nurse or something," Trisha observed as she laid out her supplies on the bench top.

"She's a…counselor of sorts. But she's completely independent of the company. She works for herself."

"She was very helpful with my friends. She must've had some kind of medical training." Trisha seemed thoughtful as she took the samples from him and began to work.

"I'm not sure. You'll have to ask her," he answered vaguely. And good luck to Kate in trying to explain that she was the priestess who served the local shifter community. "Is there anything I can do to help?" Steve changed the subject. "I'm pretty handy in the lab. I used to help my mom a bit."

"Really?" She looked at him over her shoulder, a playful expression of disbelief on her pretty face. "Do you know sterile technique?" Her tone made the question a mischievous dare.

"Does a cat scratch?" he answered in the same tone.

She laughed and handed him some of the samples she'd been transferring into centrifuge tubes.

"You know how to load that thing?" She nodded toward the nearby machine that would spin and separate the blood into its components.

Without commenting further, he expertly balanced the tubes—one on one side, then one opposite until he had the machine properly balanced. They worked together in silence for the short time it took to get all the samples prepared for separation. Trisha was using only about half of each sample, resealing the rest and packing it back in the ice they'd used to transport it. He wasn't sure what she had in mind, but it was probably better to keep some of each of the samples from the seven women in reserve so they could do more tests later, if it became necessary.

What followed was several hours spent preparing samples and analyzing data. The results were disturbing.

"Well, this is new," Trisha reported as she examined the various results she'd managed to isolate. "It's got organic and inorganic components. And a trace of silver that was probably meant to act as a catalyst. It's going to take a while to figure this out—if I *can* figure it out." She sighed heavily and leaned back against the lab bench. "But now I know why I got sick when the other girls didn't. I'm allergic to silver. Lynda is too. The rest of the gals make fun of us because they can't buy us silver jewelry for gifts. They claim we're just holding out for gold." She laughed weakly.

"Silver, huh?" Steve observed, thinking deep thoughts.

Silver was poisonous to many magical people—shifters, in particular. Apparently, fey and whatever Trisha had in her lineage was also affected by the deadly metal. Whoever had targeted the group of women—if it had been a trap designed for magic—had to have known that anything with silver in it wouldn't work as expected on magical folk. So what was the point?

Perhaps dosing them all with silver and waiting for the magic ones to self-identify? But why knock out the non-magic ones and leave the potentially more dangerous ones conscious? That seemed counterintuitive. Steve rubbed a hand over his forehead and decided to leave it for now. He'd bring the findings to Grif, Slade and the rest, and see what they thought.

In the meantime, he had a mate to protect.

She looked so defeated, her head hanging down as she leaned against the countertop. He wanted to comfort her. He wanted to take her in his arms and kiss her and tell her everything would be all right. He wanted to take her to his home, lock them both in his bedroom and make love to her until that worried exhaustion left her body completely.

But he couldn't do any of those things. Not yet. Maybe not ever. He had to approach her cautiously. Woo her.

Unfortunately, Steve had never been big on wooing. His looks and position in the Clan meant women were usually wooing *him*. There were a lot of females out there who wanted either the thrill of bedding an Alpha cat or the perceived power having him as their bed partner would create. He was second-in-command to one of the most powerful Alphas in the country. Possibly the world. Currying favor with Steve was something a lot of shifters tried to do, but he had a nose for those overtures of friendship that were genuine and those who were only seeking him out for their own benefit.

Steve moved closer to Trisha and put one hand on her shoulder, offering comfort. Not as much as he wanted to offer, but it was a start. "It'll be okay."

"No, it won't. At least not for a few days." She turned to him and suddenly they were standing very close. He could see tears in her eyes, though she seemed loathe to actually let them fall. "This compound..." she began in a soft, defeated kind of tone. "It could potentially keep them unconscious for days. This is a lot more serious than I expected. I figured—at worst—it would turn out to be some kind of date-rape drug, but this is serious anesthesia. Only it's been modified into something new and strange to me."

A tear did fall then, but she quickly wiped it away. Steve couldn't take it. He reached for her and gently pulled her into his arms. Somewhat to his surprise, she didn't resist. If anything, she clung to him for support as her lithe body trembled ever so slightly. Her head fit neatly under his chin and he felt the pressure of her cheek resting just above his heart. He'd never felt anything more perfect in his life.

She was a strong woman, but her friends had been hurt and it clearly bothered her even more than she let show. Steve understood. He'd been in her shoes, only worse. His lost friends wouldn't wake up. Ever. At least not in this realm. They'd passed beyond this mortal coil. On to bigger and better things, he hoped.

"It'll be okay. We can watch over them. We'll make them as comfortable as possible until they wake up."

"They should be in a hospital." She hiccupped and he pretended not to notice. He sensed she wouldn't want him to make a big deal out of her tears. He pulled her a little tighter and ran one hand up and down her back in a comforting gesture.

"We take care of our own around here," he said softly. If she really wanted her friends to be admitted to a human hospital, he'd have to agree, but things would be a lot less complicated if they could handle all this themselves. As the Clan usually did. "They're just sedated, right? There's no chance they could die, is there?"

If a bunch of humans died in their care, there would be hell to pay, but just nursing a few doped-up women should be all right. He'd have to rely on Clan folk to help, and it would also mean inconveniencing the wolf Pack for a bit longer than he'd hoped, but it could be done.

"No, they won't die. They're probably just going to be unconscious for a couple of days, followed by one hell of a hangover." She pulled slightly away from him to look up into his eyes. "Taking them to a hospital is going to open up a huge can of worms with their families, my family and a whole host of people you don't even want to know about." She chewed on her lower lip, worrying, and he was sorely tempted to give her lips something else to do—with his.

"They can stay where they are and we can all keep an eye on them. They're safe, which is something I can't guarantee in a hospital. Whoever tried to abduct you all might try again."

"It really was an abduction attempt?" Her gaze held even more worry and he was sorry to have put it there, but she needed to know the truth.

"There was an ambush waiting outside. I think the bar fight was started to force you all out into the street where a group of men was waiting to shove you into vans. My guys disabled the vans—and the people driving them. Without their help, I'm not sure I could've gotten all of you out safely. That kind of setup reeks of advance planning. Somebody wants one or all of you for some reason, and I aim to find out why."

"Marcia's dad is loaded. It's probably her they were after. She's the bride-to-be. She flew all of us here on her father's private jet."

Trisha didn't seem in any hurry to leave Steve's arms and he wasn't complaining. The feel of her in his embrace was doing things to him, though. Things he enjoyed…and wanted to take a whole lot further.

"Now that you're done with your lab work, I can get a better handle on the investigation. I already put some things in motion before we left the house and it's about time to check progress."

"Do you think you can find out who did this?" Suddenly, she seemed fiercer than she had. Good. He liked a strong woman who could stand up to a challenge.

"It's what I do, sweetheart." He smiled and she laughed. His boast was only a little bit over the top and just what was needed to bring a smile back to her face. He didn't like it when she wore that worried frown.

"All right then. You helped me. Now how can I help you?"

"You really want to help me?" His voice dipped low and suddenly the mood changed.

He couldn't help it. Feeling her body against him made him want things…made him want *her*. Although, all she had to do was breathe and he wanted her. He'd come to accept that fact since the moment he first caught her scent without the chemicals masking her true nature.

"Depends what you have in mind." Oh, yeah. She was rising to his challenge all right. Her playful tone and teasing smile was exactly what he'd hoped for.

"For starters…" He moved closer, dipping his head only a little to hover near hers. She didn't move away and he took it as permission to move closer. His lips hovering over hers, he whispered. "How about this?"

And then he was kissing her. Tasting her for the first time. The flavor of her kiss sent his senses spinning into overdrive as he learned the true meaning of desire. Of want. Of need.

Oh yeah, she was his. No doubt about it.

No doubt about it, Red really knew how to kiss. She allowed herself to enjoy the feel of him, the taste of him, the earthy scent of him. He was all man and he definitely knew what to do with a woman.

Trisha was oh-so-tempted to let him take all her worries away—if only just for a little while. She was out from under the watchful eye of her family and free to be with this gorgeous specimen of manhood, if she so chose. Not that she didn't indulge from time to time when she was at home, but being in a city hundreds of miles away, out of touch and out of sight, it was a lot easier.

Not to mention the fact that she'd never been so attracted to a man. Steve Redstone did something for her libido no man ever had. She'd seen him coming for her through that raucous bar brawl and that had been it. Her switch had been flipped by the raw power of the man. The dangerous prowl that announced to the world, in no uncertain terms, that he was a predator. And she most definitely wanted to be his prey.

At least for a little while. And then she wanted to do her own pouncing on him. She wanted to jump his bones so bad that she squirmed to get closer to him, running her hands over his hard muscles. She dared his tongue to duel with hers. She wanted so much…

And then her phone rang, shattering her peace. She knew that ring. It was the one she'd assigned to her brother Deke.

"Son of a bitch!" she swore, drawing away from Steve.

"What's wrong?" He seemed just a wee bit fuzzy and it made her smile. She'd made the blade lose its edge just ever so slightly. She'd done that. It made her feel powerful and feminine all at once.

"That's Deke. What am I going to tell him? He always knows when I'm lying."

"And if you let it go to voicemail?" He leaned back against the counter top while she reached for her purse and the phone it held.

"He'll just call back and then grill me about why I didn't answer it the first time he called. And before you ask, if I don't answer a third call, he'll send out the militia. In this case, I bet that would be you. He'll be calling you next if I don't answer. That said…" She had succeeded in fishing her phone out of the small bag and hit CONNECT. "Hi, Deke. How's it going?" She braced herself for the worst.

Deke was pleasant at first but then the interrogation began. He wanted to know what they'd been doing since arriving in Las Vegas and she knew she had to tread lightly. It was close to midnight and he had no doubt timed his call to check up on her.

"We went out to a club and some of the girls had a little too much to drink. We left early and they're sleeping it off. I'm just doing a few things before I turn in myself. How are things at home?" There. That was nothing but the truth—just a sanitized version of it.

Deke seemed to take her words at face value and told her a little bit about his day, then he signed off with a pleasant goodnight. He sounded pleased that his little sister had been sensible enough not to overindulge like the others and was going to bed early—and alone. Little did he know she'd probably be having sex with his friend Red on the counter top right now if not for that badly timed phone call.

She put her phone away just as another phone buzzed. It was Red's.

"He doesn't waste any time. I bet he's calling you now to confirm what I just told him. Nosy bugger." She grumbled while he reached for the small phone he wore on his hip.

"No, it's my brother, not yours," he said with one of those killer half-smiles of his, moving a few feet away to take the call.

She watched him while he talked with his brother, liking everything she saw. He was taller than her, which was important. She was usually on eye-level with most men. It was nice to have to look up a little bit. It was nice to feel small and dainty by comparison.

Sure, she felt that way with the men in her family, but this was altogether different. This was a man she was interested in—in a very earthly, sexual way. And if she was being totally honest with herself, she knew darn well she was going to do her best to get him into her bed before this visit to Las Vegas was over.

There was the sticky wicket of her brother to consider. Deke and his buddy Red, as he called him, were thick as thieves. They had a bond that went beyond mere friendship and into realms that only men who'd put their lives on the line together shared. It might not really be fair of her to expect Red to break that bond by having sex with her. Surely sleeping with your best buddy's sister was some kind of no-no in those circles, though she didn't know for certain.

Still, she wanted him. Really *wanted* him. In a way she'd never wanted a man before. It was almost a *need*. That was a startling thought, because if someone had asked her yesterday if she ever thought she'd *need* a man in her life, she would have laughed in their face. But yesterday she hadn't met

Red—or Steve, as she tried to remember to call him. With five brothers all sharing the same last name, using part of it as a nickname was bound to be confusing. Everyone she'd met so far who knew him had called him Steve. She had to remember to do the same.

He ended the call and came back over to her as she reached for the bottle of water she always had at her side. She took a sip and felt refreshed even as her temperature rose watching him pace toward her.

"Slade's got some news. We should go back if you're done here. There's an escort waiting outside to make sure we get there in one piece."

"You guys think of everything, don't you?"

"It's my job, Trisha. We'll have an escort wherever we go until we figure out who was targeting your group and why. I also want to know who, exactly, within your group was being targeted."

"Marcia—" she began, but he held up one hand, palm outward, and shook his head.

"That's the easy answer, but there are things you don't know that might have some bearing on the *real* answer. That's the one we need. The one I won't stop until I have."

"What is it I don't know?" She was perplexed by his words.

Steve sighed and ran one of those calloused hands over his hair in a gesture of frustration. "Honey, there's a lot that falls under that category, and I'm afraid it's going to be mostly up to me to enlighten you. But before I do, I want some reinforcements present. At least for the initial briefing. I think Kate could be of some help here. I'd like to defer the rest of this conversation until we're safely back at the house, if it's okay with you."

Intrigued, she really didn't want to let it go, but she saw how careful he was being about his words. Something was really bothering him. If it was bad news, maybe she didn't really want to hear it. Not now. Not while the feel of his kiss was still running like fire through her veins.

And that was another thing.

"I'm sorry Deke interrupted us." She felt a resurgence of the glow of arousal as she thought about that tempestuous kiss. It was a good distraction from the problems she still had to face…later. For now, she wanted to think about pleasanter things for a just a little while.

Steve stepped closer. "Are you really?"

She accepted the challenge of his movement and stepped right up to him, placing one hand on his shoulder and one on his chest.

"I am. Really." She leaned upward and nibbled on his chin and jaw, enjoying the feel of the sandy stubble on his cheeks against her lips. "If he hadn't interrupted us, how far would you have allowed this to go? I mean, is there some sort of guy code of honor when it comes to your friend's sister, or would you have given me what I wanted?"

He seemed to choke at her whispered words and she had to hide a smile. She was getting to him, and it was a lot easier than she'd have guessed.

"Honey, I knew from the moment I saw you in that bathrobe that Deke was going to have my head on a pike. I'll give you all you want and more. Anytime. Anywhere." He claimed her lips one more time, but this kiss was different. It was less explosive but just as passionate, only in a different way. It was more deliberate. More like a claiming than just a mere kiss.

When he drew back, they were both out of breath. She looked up into his golden eyes and made a decision. Reality could wait a few more minutes. This moment, right now, would never come again. She decided to grab onto it with both hands.

"How about here? And now?" she whispered as she reached to unbuckle his belt.

He stilled her hands by covering them with one of his. She looked up to meet his gaze, surprised he would call a halt. But the message in his eyes didn't say *stop*. No, it held something even more disturbing.

"If we do this, I need you to know it's more than just a moment out of time. It means something to me. If it doesn't mean anything to you, then I'd rather wait."

Wait? Was he kidding? When had a man ever asked to wait before having sex because he wanted it to be *meaningful?* She tilted her head and looked deep into his eyes, seeing the seriousness there.

"You really mean that, don't you?"

"With all my heart."

She sensed things were being said here without the actual words being spoken. If she had sex with him tonight, a line would be crossed. Things wouldn't be the same between them. Between him and her brother. Between her and her brother, for that matter. So the bottom line was, it had to be worth it.

Did she really think it was worth it? So much change to be with one man she'd only just met?

Her heart leapt in her chest and she knew the answer was a resounding yes. She didn't know all the changes that making love with Steven Redstone would create, but she could guess at some of them. Big changes. Was she ready for that kind of upheaval?

She'd have to be. Because the alternative—walking away without knowing his lovemaking—was untenable. Unthinkable. Truly impossible.

She needed him like she needed to breathe. She didn't understand it, but she knew it in her heart. And Trisha was famous for following where her heart led. Leaping before looking was her usual mode of transport, so why should she change now?

"It means something," she told him, whispering her words in the darkened stillness of the lab.

They were most likely alone in the building. She hadn't seen anyone on the way in. There was a naughty aspect to having sex in an office building that appealed to her wilder side.

"I don't understand it," she went on, holding his gaze as

she spoke the words that would decide her fate. "I only just met you, but there's a...connection, I guess you'd call it. Something draws me to you. Something profound and bigger than just the two of us. I don't want to deny it. I want to give into it. To embrace it. To know what it's like to be with you."

"Thank God." He looked heavenward only for a moment and then returned to stare deep into her eyes. His hands went to her shoulders and caressed her through the thin fabric of her sparkly top. "You feel it too, don't you? You feel the bond. I didn't think it would be possible, but somehow..." His words trailed off as his lips claimed hers. The kiss they shared was fierce, protective and claiming all at once. Like a wild animal staking his territory, keeping it safe from all others.

She went back to working on his belt buckle, pausing only when he lifted her stretchy top over her head. She was glad she'd packed her best undies for the trip. She knew the black lace of her bra showed off the creaminess of her skin to best advantage. He certainly seemed to appreciate it, making a sound deep in his throat that almost sounded like a growl. The smile that accompanied it told her he liked what he saw.

His belt buckle out of the way, she opened the fly of his pants, pushing downward, gasping when she discovered— much to her delight—that he wore no underwear. His hips were narrow and muscular and his cock was hard, long and nestled in a neat thatch of golden hair only a shade darker than the stuff on his head.

"Commando?" she teased, taking hold of his erection as he sucked in a breath.

She met his gaze and raised one eyebrow as she smiled. His expression held amusement and a heavy arousal that spurred her on. They were definitely on the same page. This wouldn't take long, at least not the first time.

"Saves time," he said shortly, releasing her bra clasp with one hand.

Now that took talent. She didn't want to think how much practice he'd had undressing women, but she was thankful when he pushed the straps down her arms and freed her aching breasts.

She was even more thankful when he cupped her in his palms, rubbing gently. He wasn't grabby. She liked the way he savored her skin, touching gently at first, watching and learning how she liked to be handled. She returned the favor, moving her hand over his cock in slow, squeezing motions.

"You're beautiful, Trisha," he whispered against her lips as he closed the space between them.

She was forced to let go of his cock, but he seemed intent on learning her curves with his mouth. He trailed his lips down over her breasts, pausing to lick and then suck, driving her arousal higher with each gentle nip. He opened the zipper on her short skirt and pushed it down and away, leaving her in the garter and stockings she'd chosen to wear, along with the black lace panties that matched her discarded bra.

"Yowza. You dress like a siren, Trisha mine."

She heard his words mumbled against her skin as he knelt before her, working his way down her body with hands, mouth and tongue. He expertly unhooked the stockings from the garter but didn't push them down her body. She was perplexed until she felt her panties being tugged away and the clips returned to their positions on her stockings. Apparently he wanted to fuck her with the stockings on.

A little thrill went through her when she realized he liked the way she looked in them. She did too, but nobody had ever really seen her in such feminine gear. Her usual style of dress was a lot more conservative, but the stockings had been a gift and she'd found she liked them after giving them a try. Bringing them on this trip had seemed frivolous when she was packing, but she was really glad she'd thought to pack them now.

Steve nudged her legs apart and with a shock, she realized what he wanted. How decadent she felt, standing in the middle of the lab with the most gorgeous man she'd ever met on his knees between her spread legs. His tongue touched her clit and she nearly swooned. She reached out and grabbed his head for balance, loving the texture of his short hair under her fingertips.

She could just imagine what this must look like. She was mostly naked except for her heels, garter belt and stockings. He still wore his T-shirt and pants, though they were open and his dick was sticking out like a ramrod in front. From behind though, it probably looked like he was fully dressed. Fully dressed and eating her pussy while she stood above him.

Holy moly. Just thinking about the picture they made drove her excitement level higher. And then he slid his finger into her while his tongue danced around her clit in a rapid rhythm designed to drive her insane. She cried out as she came against his mouth, her knees buckling a bit, but his free arm came around her, supporting her butt and holding her steady while he rode her through the little storm.

When she finally quieted and was able to stand on her own again, he pulled back, smiling up at her from his position on the floor. She'd never had a man look at her that way. For that matter, she'd never been given oral sex while standing up and certainly not in an empty lab in an equally empty office building. There was something appealingly naughty about all of this. The location. The setting. The man. Most definitely the man.

Steve Redstone was the sexiest man she'd ever met, and so far he'd proven to be a talented and generous lover. She couldn't wait to find out what came next.

She bent down and kissed him, loving the taste of him mixed with the faint taste of herself. She kissed him deeply, only vaguely aware of the change in height as he stood, kissing her all the while. He broke the kiss only when he bent to lift her bodily onto the cool counter top.

But she didn't mind the coolness of the clean counter under her ass. Nothing could cool down the fire that had rebuilt itself in her veins. The fire that wanted more. More of the man who had already given her a taste of what he could do.

"Slow or fast?" Steve asked as he made a place for himself between her spread thighs. She liked the way he took charge of her body, of her pleasure, but she also liked that he cared enough to ask what she wanted.

"Fast," she breathed. "Definitely fast. I don't want to wait this time. Please, don't make me wait."

He smiled that crooked smile at her and moved closer, aligning his hard cock with her wet opening. She was more than ready for him. She was desperate for him. Never before had she been so quick to go from warm to inferno for a man. Only Steve brought out the wilder side of her sexuality. There was something wild about him that met and matched the siren that rested deep in her soul.

"Your wish is my command," he teased as he moved closer still and began to slide into her. She had to change her position a bit to accommodate his large size. He went slow at first, making sure she had enough time to adjust to him. "Okay?" he asked at one point when he was about halfway in. He stopped and waited for her answer.

She clutched at his shoulders and moaned. "More," she demanded. She was beyond more than single-syllable responses. She craved him and she needed more. Why was he holding back? Couldn't he see she was desperate?

He chuckled and pushed all the way in, resting only a moment before setting up a steady rhythm she soon picked up. She met him thrust for thrust and helped as much as she could from her rather precarious perch up on the counter top. But Steve was solid as a rock. He anchored her. He took care of her. He'd make sure she wouldn't fall. She knew that much about him already and trusted him to look after her.

But she wanted more. She wanted to come. Desperately.

"Harder," she urged, moving her legs around his narrow waist, her heels bumping against his tight butt. Hot damn, the man was built.

He obliged, speeding up as well as being a little less delicate in his movements. She knew he was being careful because of their position, but she wanted him to let go.

Maybe the next time they could be in a bed and she could coax him into letting his wildman show a little more. She'd just bet he could do a lot with a bed.

She was panting as her excitement rose. His hands coaxed, stroking over her body, pausing to squeeze her nipples and then move lower. When he rubbed his fingers over her clit in time with his thrusts, all bets were off. She came hard, crying out as she convulsed around him. Only a moment later, she felt him tense and release inside her.

He hadn't worn a condom—something she insisted on with other men—but with Steve, it seemed wrong somehow. She didn't understand why the habit of a lifetime seemed unimportant, even abhorrent, in conjunction with this particular man. He was turning her world upside down and inside out, and she didn't care. She wanted it. She wanted it all. With him.

And him alone.

He clutched her to him as they both rode the wave of sensation. She felt adrift on a sea of bliss, buffeted about by the currents of satisfaction and an almost unquenchable desire. She'd never felt quite like this before.

She stiffened when his phone rang again, but he didn't leave her. In fact, he held her gaze as he reached for the phone he'd left on the counter top and answered the call.

"Hi, Deke."

Holy shit. He was talking to her brother. She wanted to squirm away but his body pinned her. His gaze pinned her as well. He stared deep into her eyes as he spoke.

"Everything's okay. I picked up surveillance as they left their hotel. They went to a club. Drank too much. Stumbled home. The end."

Steve was still inside her, a definite presence as he spoke to her brother. Shockingly, she felt her body warm to the forbidden sensations. She felt like she might come again, but she couldn't. Not while she was less than a foot away from a very sensitive microphone with her very overprotective and suspicious brother on the other end.

"Yeah, I'll keep you posted," Steve went on after her brother had said something she didn't really hear. She'd been concentrating too hard on not coming. "Sure. Talk to you tomorrow."

Steven pressed *END* very deliberately on the phone and then tossed it back onto the counter top. Still holding her gaze, he moved his fingers back down to her clit and squeezed.

That's all it took to send her over the edge one more time. She tensed and shook as he brought her another climax. He watched her throughout, only moving his hand away after the very last of the aftershocks had ended.

"You're even more beautiful when you come," he whispered. He cupped her cheek and dipped closer for a lingering kiss.

He was getting hard again within her but he pulled out. She tried to quell her disappointment. The lab setting had been fun, but she wanted to try him in a bed, and the sooner they got back to the house and found one, the better as far as she was concerned.

The lab had everything she needed to clean up. Paper towels, a sink, a biohazard disposal can. She snickered and shot him a teasing look when she threw the paper towels she'd used in there. She liked that she could make him laugh and he got her sometimes quirky sense of humor.

They left the building together, and this time, he was holding her hand. She liked the feeling, though she hadn't held hands with a boy since she was a teenager. Somehow, he made it all fresh and new. Special. Just like him.

True to his word, there were two other vehicles waiting outside for them and a few big guys at the door. He greeted them by name and nodded at them while he ushered her back to his vehicle. He opened her door and helped her get settled, stealing a quick kiss before sealing her inside the SUV. When he climbed in behind the steering wheel, the other guys piled into their dark vehicles too. Within moments, they were all heading back the way they'd come—one escort vehicle in front and one behind theirs.

"So those guys work for you?" she asked, curious about the huge men who were even now guarding their path.

"Yeah. They're all good friends too. And just so you know, they were guarding us on the way here too, you just didn't see them. I wanted a chance to explain the danger to you first, before you knew I was having us watched. It was also a good demonstration at my boys' stealth capabilities."

"Wow, you're right. I didn't see them at all." She looked out the window at the very big, very obvious vehicles. How could she have missed them before?

"That was the point," he answered, a little smug. "They're good at what they do and you can trust them to look out for you. Quite a few of them served with your brother too," he added, frowning.

"My brother." Now that was a subject sure to put a downer on things.

"Yeah." Steve sighed as he turned a corner, casually checking his mirrors. "We're going to have to talk about him sooner or later. All the guys in our unit knew how he was about you. Protective in the extreme."

"*Over*-protective, you mean." She leaned her head back against the headrest and closed her eyes briefly. "I guess it all stems from our childhood. When his dad died, it shook his world, I think. Then a few years later, Mom remarried. By the time I was born, Mom says Deke's protective instincts had really ratcheted into high gear, even though he was only a kid. He loved his dad—followed him into the Army despite the admiral's influence—but Deke bonded with my dad more than any of them ever expected. They're two peas in a pod. Cut from the same cloth. Whatever cliché you want to use. They're two very scary dudes when they're in circle-the-wagons mode, and they're chauvinists through and through."

"I didn't realize you were half-siblings." Steve said and then got really quiet. Maybe it was just the dark of the night closing in around them, but the mood in the small cabin of the vehicle suddenly changed from casual to alert.

"Yeah. Does it make a difference?"

"Not to me," he was quick to assure her. "But it could explain a few things."

"Like what?" She turned to watch him, concerned when she saw the muscle ticking in his jaw.

"It's all part of what I need to tell you, but I'd rather wait until we're back at the house. Your dad, was he Special Forces too? Is that what you mean about him being an influence on Deke?"

She had no idea why he was being so mysterious and it worried her a little, but she was willing to answer his questions. For now. But the time was soon coming when she'd demand a few answers of her own.

"Yeah, Dad's a Navy SEAL. Mom has a thing for military guys, I guess. Deke's dad was Army, so he decided to shoot for Green Beret. The only thing he doesn't share with my dad is his affinity for water. Dad swims like a fish. Deke sorta sank a lot when he was younger. He overcame it, but it wasn't a natural skill for him."

"Your father is Admiral Morrow?" Steve asked, as if only just realizing the connection.

"Yeah. Deke took his last name when Dad officially adopted him soon after my folks got married. Why?"

"Because I've heard Deke deny any connection to the admiral. One time someone asked him about it and he insisted that the last name was just a coincidence." Steven gave her that raised-eyebrow look that spoke volumes.

"Well, I know Deke doesn't like getting special treatment because of who he's related to. The higher-ups must know, but he probably doesn't want the guys he works with day-to-day looking at him differently because of it."

"I guess so," Steve replied noncommittally.

She sighed and looked out the window, squinting her eyes as they crossed a road. There was a big pickup truck on the side street moving way too fast.

"Red?" was all she had time to say before their vehicle was hit by the other one and spun out of control.

Time slowed as the fact that they'd just been rammed by a truck filtered though her shocked mind. It had hit the rear of their SUV and put them into a spin. A few feet sooner and she'd have been in the impact zone.

Information came at her hard and fast. They were spinning down the side street. The truck had pushed them across the intersection and into a much smaller industrial road. The place was deserted and the quick glimpses she got of the two escort vehicles as she spun around and around told her that they were being waylaid by two more trucks that had come out of nowhere.

This is an ambush, she thought hysterically as the SUV started to tip over wildly.

Then it rolled. Someone was screaming and she realized belatedly it was her.

The sturdy SUV held together and she thanked God she had worn her seatbelt. They came to a stop on their side, her door on the pavement. Steve cut through his seatbelt even before they came to a complete stop, using a knife he'd taken from his boot. He was all action, removing weapons from compartments she hadn't known about. He handed her a big, black handgun and silently flipped the safety off.

"Just in case," he whispered. He didn't ask if she knew how to shoot. She did, of course. Every person in her family could handle weapons. Dad had made certain of that. "Stay here and whatever you see, don't shoot me, okay?"

He gave her a wink that made her want to smile despite the desperate situation. Then he vaulted out of the broken window on his side of the car, which was now facing the sky. She craned her neck to see out the broken window, but the safety glass of the windshield had shattered and held, for the most part. It was really hard to see anything through it.

Trisha worked on getting herself free of the seat belt. It took some doing, but she was finally able to move. And that's when she saw the blood. Her leg was bleeding from a long gash that had ruined her stocking. She couldn't tell how deep it was. Her leg felt mostly numb, so the pain wasn't really registering. Maybe it would later. But she realized she ought to tie something around her leg, just in case the gash was worse than she hoped. She wiggled out of the ruined stocking and used it to tie a tourniquet around her thigh. Now *that* hurt, but it was better to be safe than...well...dead from blood loss.

As she worked, she heard a lot of strange noises from outside. Yelling and...growling? Then screaming. A few sporadic gunshots in the distance. The sound of motors revving and moving away at a fast clip. Then silence.

She tried to see out the window but the fragmented images made no sense. She saw a cat. A really big cat. And it had blood dripping from its fangs and claws as it padded toward her. And then it...morphed. It changed as it moved into an upright, bipedal shape that was absolutely immense. It was like something out of a horror movie and then it...

She must've lost more blood than she thought. She was hallucinating.

# CHAPTER FIVE

Steve paused to pick up his pants and discarded shirt. He put the pants on and used the dirty T-shirt to wipe the blood off his face and hands. He'd had to use all his abilities to hold off the attackers until his men could fight their way free and come to his aid. They'd managed to run off their attackers, but it had been a close thing.

Steve had taken a few bites out of the bad guys. He'd know their stink if he encountered any of those men ever again. But they'd buggered off before any of them could be captured and questioned. It was frustrating. There were a lot of questions he wanted to ask those guys, but it looked like he wouldn't get the chance this night.

He headed back to the ruined SUV and its precious cargo.

"It's okay. They're gone," he called out, wanting to make sure she knew not to shoot him. "Let's get you out of there."

"Red?" Her voice quavered and he was surprised by her reaction. He'd thought she was tougher. But it didn't matter. He was plenty tough enough for both of them.

He poked his head into the driver's door, which was now on top. And then the scent of blood hit him strong. *Oh, no.*

"Are you hurt, baby?" *Son of a bitch.* He should never have left her alone. But he'd thought she was okay. Guilt swamped him.

"My leg," she whispered. "I think I've lost a lot of blood. I saw a cat. And then it was you."

She sounded hurt, confused and frightened. He grimaced. The last thing he'd wanted to do was make her afraid of his inner beast.

"It's okay, sweetheart. The cat's gone. I'm here. I'll take care of you." He reached in and lifted her out by placing his hands under her arms. She helped as best she could, but she was weak. And from the strong scent of her blood, she really had lost quite a bit.

He pulled her up and out and into his arms, noting the nylon tourniquet she'd fashioned out of her stocking. Good girl. The bleeding had slowed, but wasn't quite stopped and that worried him.

"Rory, get Kate on the phone and have her meet us at the Pack house," he ordered one of his men, moving as quickly as possible toward one of the cars that had been escorting them. They'd sustained minimal damage and one was a large SUV that would easily fit him and Trisha in the back seat. "Get us out of here, quick as you can. Trisha's hurt and has lost a lot of blood."

"Emergency kit's in the back," Rory quickly reminded him as they all piled into the big vehicle.

Rory was a good man to have around in an emergency. He was a man of few words, but those few were exactly the ones you needed to hear. In this case, Steve was glad to know they had supplies and he could start fixing Trisha up even before they made it to the safety of the Pack house. Rory also drove like a bat out of hell. Which was just what Steve wanted right now. The fastest, safest route, and a competent would-be race car driver.

Steve took a closer look at Trisha's leg as they drove. He'd laid her across the bench seat and taken a position by her feet, raising her legs and letting them rest on his thighs. Feet up was a good position for shock and it might slow the bleeding.

He took a look and was surprised by the jagged gash that

was way deeper than he'd thought.

"I'm glad you got this tourniquet on here, baby," he whispered. "Don't worry. We'll get you fixed up in no time."

"Is it bad?" she asked. "I couldn't really see the wound in the dark."

"I've seen worse." Not often, but he had. "It'll be okay." He sent prayers heavenward that he wasn't telling a lie.

Steve looked out the window to get a read on where they were and realized they had a closer alternative. Making a quick decision, he reached for his phone even as he spoke to their driver.

"Go to my place, Rory. It's a lot closer. I'll call Kate."

Putting actions to words, he dialed Slade's number, knowing Kate would be with him. Slade agreed to the redirect and said they'd meet him at Steve's house. He'd even send around some of their men to secure the location before they got there. One less thing for Steve to worry about.

He dug into the supplies in the emergency kit and found a couple of units of saline. He put those aside. He didn't want to be inserting needles into her veins in a moving vehicle, but it was good to know he had fluids on hand if she needed them.

"How you doing, Doc?" he asked her, watching her closely for signs she was in trouble.

"I'm okay. The leg is starting to burn. Do you have any water? Did you bring my bag? I always have a bottle in there."

He had snagged her pocketbook on one arm as he took her out of the mangled SUV and had thrown it onto the floor of this vehicle. He dug around until he located it and fished inside until he laid his hands on the cool plastic bottle inside. Sure enough, it was a water bottle. He unscrewed the cap and handed it to her as she tried to push herself up.

She took the bottle from his hand and he moved to support her back so she could rise up enough to take a few sips. And then, as she started to drink the water, the strangest thing happened.

Where she'd been on the verge of passing out, suddenly she seemed to gain energy right before his eyes. She stopped trembling. As she downed the water, her color returned. And when he looked at her wound, it seemed to look a bit better than it had just a moment ago.

Water had done that.

And then he realized what she was. Or what one of her ancestors must have been. Some kind of water nymph. Judging by the way she drew him, maybe a sea siren.

Steve had to smile. Sea sirens were said to lure sailors to their death. Well, he wasn't a sailor and he had a little magic of his own. She definitely lured him to her, but he didn't think it was to kill him. Unless he could die from pleasure.

Seeing how the water healed her, he thought he knew what she needed. And he had just the thing back at his house.

Rory drove like a maniac, and before long they were pulling up in front of his place. Steve had built his own home near enough to his brothers to be on hand when needed, but far enough away to have a little room of his own to prowl. The house had taken a long time to finish, as Steve had done most of the work himself, and he was really proud of how it had come out.

One of his favorite features was out back and he was going to take Trisha there first thing. He carried her in his arms from the SUV and walked straight up the garden path that would take him behind the house.

"Where are we going?" She was much more alert since she'd had the water. If his guess was right, she'd be even better in a few minutes.

"I think there's something you need to see—and experience." He walked around back and triggered one of many motion sensors he'd installed.

The backyard was flooded with low illumination from the many accent lights he'd put in. The whole place glowed in rich yellows and oranges with a few brighter spots. At the center of the wide backyard was his target. An exceptionally large swimming pool.

RED

Steve had opted for a sand-colored bottom to the pool rather than the more traditional neon blue. He wanted his waterscape to blend more with the desert around him. A wooden pergola shaded one end of the custom-shaped island of water in the middle of the desert.

"Oh, that is lovely."

Steve heard the catch in her voice, the little breathless yearning that filled her tone when she caught sight of the water. She wanted in. He could see it in the way her gaze fixated on the pool and never wavered as he walked nearer.

"It's salt water," he whispered.

"Mmm." The sound she made seemed almost involuntary. She reacted as if he'd just said something naughty and he could feel her body reaching out toward the oasis he'd created in his backyard.

Steve walked them around to the shallow end where he'd created a set of wide stairs that led down into the water. It was his favorite place to hang out and just think, sitting on the steps, floating, letting the water soothe him in the hot desert sun.

Without pausing, he walked right down the steps, into the water. He was still barefoot and bare-chested from when he'd shifted to fight. He'd only taken time to put his pants back on and nothing in the pockets was in danger from the water except his phone. He paused when the water was about mid-thigh on him and lowered Trisha's feet into the water so he could free up one hand to fish out his phone and toss it into the cushion of greenery to one side of the pool. He'd retrieve it later. For now, he had to see to his woman.

Trisha's skin started to take on a pearly sheen as her feet touched the water. Her eyes closed and expression of bliss came over her face. She was fully clothed except for the one stocking that was still acting as a tourniquet, but even as he watched, the need for the tight band around her leg lessened.

"I thought so. Water is your element," he commented with a pleased feeling.

Her eyes shot open and she looked afraid as she met his

gaze. He did his best to calm her.

"Don't worry, sweetheart. Your secret is safe with me."

"How did you know to bring me to water?" She seemed terrified that he'd somehow figured out what made her so different from other people.

"The water bottles in your bag were my first clue, but please don't look so scared." He used his free hand to brush strands of her hair out of her face. "There's so much I have to tell you, and believe me when I say, I love the fact that you're part nymph."

"My dad says *sprite*. He says we're descended from a water sprite."

"I would have said sea siren," he teased. "You have certainly put me under your spell." He dipped his head to kiss her lightly.

But he couldn't afford to get too distracted. She was still injured. He thought he knew the cure, but they still had to go that final step. Steve lifted his head and walked deeper into the pool.

"If we submerge the wound, will it heal completely?" he asked, watching her and her wound carefully.

She nodded tightly, still nervous even after her admission. She knew she was special. She knew she had magic running through her veins. Things were looking up. Maybe she would be able to accept the fact that she was his mate and that he was a shifter. But first they had to get her well and functioning on two solid legs again. If he guessed right, that would happen momentarily. And then they could move on to more pleasurable things.

He kept his arm around her shoulders as he walked her deeper in to the pool. Her legs floated at first. She seemed to be trying to keep the injury above water. Maybe she was still afraid for him to see her magic? She'd learn to trust him. This was the first step.

He paused and let her make the decision. Slowly, she lowered her legs one at a time. First the uninjured one, then the one with the nasty gash that had already grown smaller

RED

from when he'd first seen it back at the crash site.

When the lower edge of the gash touched the water it immediately cleared and sealed, leaving unblemished skin behind. As her leg sank deeper into the water, the phenomenon continued until she stood before him on two perfectly formed, uninjured legs. He'd never seen anything like it.

Sure, shifters healed fast, but nothing like this. It was miraculous. And fantastic. He'd worried about her recovery, but there wasn't going to be any recovery. She was already healed.

Trisha bent down to untie the tourniquet. "Guess I don't need this anymore," she mumbled. Then she looked up at him, her gaze filled with uncertainty. "Did I just freak you out?"

Steve couldn't hold back his smile. "Not in the least. I think it's wonderful that you're so magical."

Her head tilted upward as she squinted at him. "You're taking this awfully well."

"Yeah, I am, aren't I?" His grin got bigger and he sank into the pool, washing the grime of the fight away from his skin. "Why do you suppose that is?"

"You've seen someone like me before?" Her tone was hopeful but very tentative.

"Actually, no. But I've seen—and done—similar things in my time. We're very much alike, you and I. We've both been touched by magic."

Now she looked really intrigued. "Magic?"

"What else would you call spontaneous healing when you come into contact with water?"

She sighed and ran her hands through the water, making soothing ripples. "Yeah, I guess you're right. So what kind of magic can you do?"

"Well, do you remember the big cat you talked about seeing at the crash site?"

She shuddered and he tried not to wince. She seemed afraid of his cat, which the beast inside him didn't like at all.

71

"I thought I was hallucinating from blood loss."

"You weren't. There was a cougar there, fighting the guys who were trying to abduct you—again."

"But I saw..." She trailed off, shock covering her features. "The cougar was *you!*"

She backed away from him, but he reached out and caught her shoulder to pull her body into his, wrapping his arms around her as the water supported them both. He was standing about waist-high in the shallows.

"I'm *were*, honey. In fact, pretty much everyone you've met since we left the bar has been like me. It's not something we advertise, but since you're magical too, it's okay. Don't tell me you've never met a *were* before."

She shook her head. *"*Not to my knowledge. What's a *were*, exactly? Does everybody I met turn into big, lethal cats?"

"No. Not at all." She seemed to relax slightly at his words. "Only a few of us are cougars. Slade is a panther and the rest of the guys you met are wolves. I took you and your friends to the wolf Pack house. It was the only place I knew that was equipped to handle that many people, but the Alpha wasn't too pleased with me bringing so many humans into the heart of his Pack's territory."

"Wolves," she repeated. "You mean like werewolves? They're real?" Her voice rose on each successive word as she took it all in.

"Oh, they're real all right. Just like me." He heard faint noises from the house.

He'd known there were a few guards standing sentry around his property and he'd seen a few moving shadows on the way into the yard. He hadn't been alarmed. He had recognized their scents. They were friends. But the newcomer to the house was louder. Less stealthy. Had to be Kate, the priestess.

"We'll talk more about this, but we're about to have company. Kate's here."

Trisha looked around in surprise as Kate opened the

RED

sliding glass door that led into the house. Kate had a look of concern on her face and her eyes widened as she drew nearer.

"Water? That's her element?" Kate asked, stopping by the side of the pool.

"How—" Trisha was at a loss.

"Well, you look fine now, but judging by the frantic phone call from the big guy..." Kate gestured with her thumb toward Steve, "...I'd say you were in bad shape a few minutes ago. I'm glad you're better. Is there anything I can help with?"

"No, thanks. I'll be fine now. I just needed the water," she admitted, though it felt really strange to talk about her unique abilities out loud with anyone other than her father.

"Yeah, I can see that. It makes your aura glow in shades of blue and green. It's really beautiful," Kate said, looking at Trisha, but not at her face. Instead, the other woman was gazing at Trisha's arms and legs and the water that gave her life and energy.

"Kate here can actually *see* magic," Steve told her. "That is one of her many talents."

"Are you a werewolf too?" Trisha felt compelled to ask. She still couldn't quite believe everything Steve had told her—or the fact that she'd seen a giant mountain lion transform into a very naked and buff Steve Redstone less than an hour ago.

Kate laughed. "No. I'm the local priestess. I serve the Lady. The Mother Goddess that magical folk tend to believe in. I have some magic skills of my own, but I can't shapeshift. I leave all that to my husband."

Kate gestured behind her and suddenly Slade was there. He'd moved into the yard so silently that Trisha couldn't really be sure when he'd shown up. The guy was spooky and scary in a way that Steve wasn't—even after seeing his alter-ego cat with blood dripping from its teeth and claws. Trisha didn't know what to make of that. This was all too much. She held on to Steve for support as a wave of dizziness washed over her.

The water was healing her, but she'd still lost quite a lot of

73

blood. It would take time for the water and its magic to replace it.

"The guys are going over the ambush scene. Your SUV is a total loss, but you knew that already. Tough break, Steve," Slade murmured. "I'll go out there as soon as I can to see if there are any magical traces."

"I wouldn't expect any. The guys I fought pretty much wet their pants when they saw our animal sides. I don't think they knew they were going up against shifters," Steve said. "Maybe hired guns. Human. No magic that I could see."

"But somehow they knew which vehicle to strike," Slade countered.

"We weren't being coy," Steve responded. "I had Trisha with me in the center vehicle. Guards front and back. It was an obvious target, but I thought the extra firepower of having two escort vehicles would be enough deterrent."

"Apparently someone wants to get their hands on your new friend bad enough to send a strike force," Slade observed. "Any idea why?"

All eyes turned to Trisha, but she was at a loss. "I have no idea," she protested. "I only came here to go to a bachelorette party. I didn't know anything about you guys until just now, and the only other person I've ever known who had abilities like mine is my dad. Seriously, I'm new to all this." She wanted to protest her innocence some more, but Steve's hand on her back soothed her, letting her know without words that he understood.

"Well, we are in a desert," Kate observed with a wry twist of her lips. The uncomfortable attention left Trisha as the focus shifted to Kate and their puzzle. "You have to admit, finding a water nymph out here is kind of unique. If someone could harness her power, they could do a quite a bit of damage with it. Or good…though I doubt anyone who wanted to do good with her abilities would try to take them by force."

"I'm not a nymph," Trisha muttered. "Dad says we're sprites. Water sprites. Or at least part, anyway. Mom is human."

"Which brings up another question," Slade cut in. "Why isn't Deke magical? I've worked with him several times and I never caught a whiff of magic around him. Not once. What gives?"

"Different fathers," Steve said shortly and Slade nodded as if those two simple words explained everything.

Well, they did. Essentially. But it didn't encompass all the sorrow and joy that went with the loss of Deke's father and the gaining of a new dad when a certain Navy SEAL married his widowed mom.

"Does Deke know?" Slade asked.

"Yeah. It's a little hard to hide. But Dad swore him to secrecy."

"No wonder he didn't make much of a fuss when he saw me slip up a few times," Steve seemed to think aloud. "Most guys would've asked why I could hear things they couldn't, or smell things so faint only animal-enhanced senses could pick it up. But Deke never batted an eye. Oh, he might've raised an eyebrow at me a few times, but he never came out and asked. He respected my desire for privacy and it's allowed us to have a really good friendship." Steve stroked her shoulder. "Which is all going to disappear when I tell him I've fallen for his little sister."

"Maybe not." She tried to be positive, but she'd always known Deke was going to have a hard time with any man she decided to get serious with.

Slade laughed out loud. "Good luck with that," he scoffed with a smile. "But in the meantime, we need to figure out who is after you and put a stop to it. Your safety is job one right now, so I expect you to stick to Steve here like glue. Got it?"

Slade's tone was teasing, but Trisha understood that he meant every word. It only made sense. She knew she needed protection while this threat persisted. She also needed their help in discovering who was targeting her.

"I will. But I want to be in on the investigation. I don't

want to be left out in the cold, out of the loop, wondering what's going on. Do we have an agreement? I want to know what you know and expect to be kept updated."

She looked from Slade to Steve and back again, knowing that both of them had to agree—though Steve's approval was more important to her than anything else. She wanted him to respect her wishes and abilities. She wanted him to trust her. Maybe it was asking too much on such short acquaintance, but still, she wanted it.

"Done." Steve didn't hesitate, and it warmed her heart.

She looked over at Slade and he nodded slowly. Good. They weren't going to treat her like a good little girl and keep her in the dark. That was a victory for her. All too often, Deke did that to her. He treated her like the child he had protected. But she wasn't that child anymore, and her big brother was going to have to come to terms with that sooner or later. Probably sooner now that she and Steve had gotten together.

Where they would go from here relationship-wise, she didn't know, but she definitely wanted more of the amazing sex they'd shared back in the lab. Sex and even the casual affection he'd displayed since. She wanted the closeness. The camaraderie. The companionship. And maybe…just maybe…love?

It was very possible she was already in love with him, but she didn't really know if he felt the same. She was afraid to probe in case she scared him away. She had to tread lightly and see where it all would lead.

"Well, it looks like you don't really need me." Kate rubbed her hands together and smiled. "I'll head back to the Pack house and keep an eye on your friends. They were all still resting comfortably when I left. There's been no change, really. One of the werewolf women is a registered nurse. She's going to help me watch them. They should be good until morning—which is only a few hours away at this point. We can reevaluate then and decide what to do from there. Sound good?"

"Yeah, that'll have to do," Trisha agreed.

She was energized by the water but she did need to sleep sometime. Fatigue was catching up with her, even as the water healed her.

"We'll stay here overnight," Steve added, talking mostly to Slade. "Rory's squad is on the perimeter and Gunter's on the roof. I don't think they'll try for her inside the heart of our territory, but the house is well-defended."

"Good enough," Slade agreed. "I'll deploy the rest of the guys and handle things while you take care of your lady."

"Thanks, buddy." Steve sounded grateful and she realized that Slade was probably doing Steve's job.

He was covering for Steve so he could stay with her. And Steve sounded really grateful for the favor. Maybe he was starting to feel things for her too? She really hoped so. The signs were very positive in that direction at the moment.

"Do you mind if I swim a little? It relaxes me. And don't worry if I stay under for a long time. I don't need to breathe as often as most people." Gosh, it still felt strange to talk so openly about her abilities, but she liked it. She liked not having to hide who she really was from him.

"Sure. Enjoy yourself." He leaned in and gave her a quick, gentle kiss before letting her go so she could swim free. "Just don't overdo it."

She looked back at him as she began to tread away toward the deeper end. "This really is a lovely pool. I'm glad it's salt water. A regular pool wouldn't have been nearly as helpful. The chlorine can be hard to deal with."

"I can imagine," he said noncommittally, leaning back against the wide steps, immersing his bare chest. She couldn't see it in the dim light, but she knew the blood from her now-sealed wound had gotten into the pool.

"I'm sorry for the blood in the water." She looked around, searching for the machinery she knew had to be hidden somewhere that kept the water so clean and pure. "Will it mess things up?"

"Nah. It'll be okay. I installed a heavy duty system here.

It's more powerful than most backyard swimming pools. By morning the water will be fully cycled and any residue will be filtered away. It's all good."

She nodded and walked deeper into the water, thinking about that. This entire setup was like something out of a magazine devoted to billionaires' mansions. The pool was no cookie-cutter design either. It had been given a floor and walls that had an almost sandy texture to them. They were also the color of sand. No neon-aqua-blue pool here. This was definitely unique. And there were no sharp angles. Everything flowed as if nature had put it here. There were plantings all around in strategic places and on one side it looked like there was a waterfall that could be turned on.

The lighting was subtle too. Muted yellows and oranges illuminated the scene but kept the atmosphere intimate while deterring bugs. Very nice. And she couldn't find any trace of the machinery that kept the water in such fine condition. Maybe under the waterfall? She stretched out and began a leisurely swim toward that end of the pool. She could see everything under the crisp, clear water because there was underwater lighting placed very discretely, but so that it illuminated every point along the large body of water.

It was really amazing. And gorgeous. She would never have imagined something like this could exist out here in the desert. He must have to add water all the time because the heat probably made it evaporate quickly. Or maybe the framework she saw above as she floated on her back was more than just decorative? Maybe it allowed for some kind of covering during the daylight hours?

She wanted more than anything to see this place in daylight. She'd bet it was even more beautiful when she could really see the intricate patterns in the tile work on the patio and the true colors of the vegetation all around.

Red—make that Steve, she corrected herself—had to be really well off financially if he could afford to build a place like this. Of course, Redstone Construction was one of the most successful companies of its kind. And he was a

Redstone, after all. She hadn't really thought about it before, but he must be loaded.

And he had an eye for beauty and design. From the way he talked, he had built the place. It was his home. He had selected how it would look. And she loved everything he'd done with it. If this backyard was anything to judge by, they had very similar taste.

All things in his favor. It didn't hurt that he was also irresistibly handsome, smart and fierce to boot. Steve was the complete package. So far, there wasn't anything she'd seen him do, or heard him say, that turned her off.

Okay, the whole turning-into-a-cat-and-clawing-people thing was a little hard to take, but she had her own unique abilities that set her apart too. At least with him, she could be completely honest about those abilities. She'd never been able to tell anyone about any of the things she could do. In fact, she'd had to go out of her way on many occasions to act *normal*, so her friends and boyfriends wouldn't realize there was anything different about her. That had been a real drag sometimes.

With Steve, she could be who she really was and she didn't have to hide anything. The idea was liberating. And very, very seductive.

# CHAPTER SIX

Steve watched her swim, and damn if she wasn't the most graceful thing he'd ever seen in the water. Even wearing the short skirt and top she'd been in all evening—except when they'd been fucking like bunnies in the lab—she swam gracefully.

Which reminded him. He had to get someone to transfer some of her things to his place. There was no question in his mind that she wouldn't be going back to the hotel. Someone was targeting her. After tonight's second ambush, there could be no doubt. He'd have to figure out what it was about her that made her such a hot target.

Besides the obvious, of course. She was beautiful and by all accounts, very magical. He couldn't *see* magic the way Slade and his mate could, but the way she responded to water was a very obvious thing.

It had been a hell of a long day. He needed to get the investigation moving, but he also needed to get some shuteye. She, especially, needed sleep, and he would see to it that she got it…eventually. He had big plans for the two of them and his king-size bed first, but once he took the edge off, he'd let her sleep. Safe and sound, in his arms. Skin to skin. Body to body. As it should be.

But he had a few things to settle first, before he could get them both to that special place where only the two of them existed. He moved out of the pool and reached for the phone he'd discarded on the ground. He punched one of the speed dial numbers while Trisha submerged and seemed to swim around like some sort of mermaid in the deep end of the pool. She stayed under a long time and if she hadn't warned him she might, he would have gone in and fished her out. As it was, he had time to make a few calls.

First, he updated his brother Grif on the events of the night. Then he started gathering intel from his men and doling out assignments. He sent some of his female security detail out to get Trisha and her friend's things from the hotel. He instructed them to bring Trisha's stuff to his house. She would need her clothes and toiletries if she was going to stay here.

Eventually, Trisha's head broke the surface of the water again. He'd timed it and she'd been under for at least twenty minutes. She wasn't breathing hard so he imagined she probably could have stayed under longer. Amazing.

She swam toward him, making barely a ripple in the water. She seemed to be part of the water. At one with it.

She stood when she reached the shallower end and began walking toward him. As she rose out of the water, she…dried. It was the darnedest thing he'd ever seen. Before she was even on the first step, her hair was flowing, long and clean down her back. Completely dry. As were her clothes and skin as she continued up the steps out of the pool.

"Now that's a nifty trick," Steve commented as she sauntered toward him, holding his gaze. She smiled and the knowing look in her eyes sent his libido into overdrive.

"I showed you mine, now why don't you show me yours? Can you let the cat out to play?" She stopped right in front of his chair, looking down at him with a challenging light in her expressive eyes. The water had reenergized her, all right. It had also made her daring and bold. Two things he liked in women, as a rule.

"Are you sure? You seemed afraid of my other half before.

I don't want to scare you."

"Show me what you got, tiger," she dared him and he hoped it wasn't all bravado.

Standing, he crowded her a bit as he unbuttoned his sodden pants. Unlike her, he wasn't able to magically dry off. He dropped trou and stood before her, hard, as he had been almost constantly since first catching her real, unmasked scent.

Naked, he moved a short distance away to let her get the full effect. He called on the cat that lived inside his soul and changed. He didn't linger in the half-cat, half-human battle form he'd used to fight those bastards earlier in the evening. He figured that'd be the hardest for her to handle if she really was still apprehensive about his kitty side.

He went straight to the big cat form—the resolution of his shift from human to cat. He was big as a man and his cat form was just as large. Way more massive than most wild cougars, he was proud of his stature and knew he looked reasonably good in both his forms.

He yawned, showing his teeth to her, watching her carefully to see if she was frightened. She seemed more fascinated than scared, so he padded over to her, prowling closer until he could rub against her legs like a much smaller cat would. She ran her fingers through his fur and he purred deep within his chest, the sound vibrating out into the darkness.

This woman was everything he wanted in a mate—and then some. He'd never really counted on having a mate of a different magical species. If he found one, he figured she'd be another cougar. He hadn't ever expected to meet an Other that flipped his switch so entirely.

There was no doubt inside him. She was his and he was hers. The whole nymph thing be damned. He knew his own mind and the cat that shared his soul was purring *mate*, over and over. That cat recognized her. And he'd never known his cat's instincts to be wrong. Ever.

"Your fur is so soft," she marveled, stroking his flanks as

he twined around her legs.

She giggled and he knew she wasn't afraid of him. Good. They were making progress.

He nudged her toward the glass door that led into the house and she laughingly complied, picking up her ever-present bag along the way. He carried his cell phone in his mouth, which wasn't ideal but would do for now.

She opened the door and let him precede her inside, then shut it behind them.

He didn't waste time on the ground floor. He knew Slade and the other security guys had checked it out already. And Steve trusted his nose—and his security measures—enough to know that no bad surprises lurked in his own home.

He ushered Trisha toward the stairs and padded upward behind her, then nosed in front to lead her to his bedroom door. It was a simple matter to reach up and open the levered door handle. Most shifter households had handles rather than knobs. They were just easier to manipulate if one didn't want to shift to get inside.

Steve dropped his cell phone on the night stand next to his bed before turning to face Trisha. He made sure she was watching as he shifted form, holding the scarier battle form for a moment this time, allowing her to get a good look at all phases of his shift. She seemed fascinated rather than petrified, judging from her expression and the subtle nuances of her delectable scent. Good. She wasn't afraid of the cat or the beast.

When he was a man again, she walked forward into his arms as if she belonged there. And she did. She laid her head against him, her cheek over his heart.

"You're an amazing guy, Red," she whispered and his heart expanded, taking in her words. They made him feel warm. Almost…loved.

Was it too soon to hope that his magical mate felt something for him besides the rather obvious desire? Lust, he understood, but he hoped for love. Craved it with every fiber of his being, when he'd never wanted any of his bedmates to go that final step before.

Love was permanent. Everlasting. Divine.

He wanted that with Trisha, and he knew in his heart that he already loved her. Now the question was, could she reciprocate?

"You're pretty amazing yourself, Doc." He stroked her back, loving the way she fit against him. "Only thing is, you're overdressed, honey."

She giggled. "Yeah, I guess I am, aren't I?" She pulled away and would have begun undressing, but he wanted to do it.

"Allow me," he rumbled, his voice dropping into an almost-purr that he couldn't quite control. She seemed to like it, so he moved closer, taking over the task of removing her clothes. He'd done some of it before, in the lab, but he'd been in too much of a rush then to truly appreciate her beauty.

This time, he took his time, running his fingers over her skin, then following with his lips and tongue…until she was moaning in pleasure and writhing against him. When he finally had her completely bare, he stepped back, admiring his handiwork. Her clothes lay strewn around her feet on the floor and her lithe, bare body beckoned to him. Demanded his possession in the most subtle way.

Steve backed up, taking a seat on the edge of the big bed and just watched her for a moment. She began to squirm a bit under his scrutiny and he realized she wasn't comfortable enough with him yet to play this particular game. Soon though, he promised himself. He'd do his best to convince her of how beautiful she was to him and how much he enjoyed just looking at her gorgeous body. For now, he'd move slowly. Let her learn him step by step, as he learned her.

Or maybe not. He finally realized, as much as he was looking at her, she was also looking at him. Unbidden, she moved forward, her gaze focused on his cock, standing straight and hard, ready for her. Without so much as a word, she reached out, grasping him as he gasped at her sudden movement.

And then all thoughts of going slow left his mind as she straddled his hips and sank down onto him, her hand guiding them together in the most amazing way. The pressure of her fingers was replaced by the warm, wet pressure of her body as she sank onto his cock, taking him balls deep in one long, sensuous stroke.

Adjusting her position by grabbing his shoulders and sinking lower onto his lap, she finally met his gaze, a smile of impassioned deviltry on her face. She was in control here, contrary to what he might've believed before. This was a woman who knew damn well what she wanted and wasn't afraid to reach out and grasp it. Steve, for one, was all in favor of that.

"Is it okay?" she asked, a moment of uncertainty showing on her lovely face.

"Nothing has ever been this okay in my entire life. Honey, you can slide your pussy down over me anytime, anywhere." His voice was almost a growl, but she didn't seem to mind.

"Be careful, big guy. I might just take you up on that."

Her playfulness made him think sinful thoughts. "Oh, I like the sound of that."

"Good, because I like the way you fill me, Red." She let out a gasp as he shifted, jostling her over him. He needed a better hold.

"You want to ride or would you rather I did all the work? Is your leg up for this?" Concern knitted his brow as he remembered the injury she'd sustained.

"My leg is fine," she answered off-handedly. "Why don't you lay down? I think I'll give this a try."

He laid back, helping her settle into a better position over him, loving the friction as they moved together and apart, adjusting their position. Damn. This was going to be so good.

And then she began to move. Slowly at first, hesitant in a way that told him she hadn't done this a lot. She gripped his shoulders, then found her balance and sat up, deepening the penetration and changing the angle. *Oh, yeah.*

He watched her breasts jiggle above him and he couldn't help but reach upward to tease her nipples and then stroke down over her soft skin with his fingers. He held her hips, reached around to squeeze her luscious fanny, then moved forward to find the little button at the juncture of her thighs that made her moan.

Steve rubbed her clit, loving the way she said his name as her pleasure mounted. When she climaxed on him, he almost came with her, but he had other ideas. He held it, knowing he'd have his chance, and it would be even better for waiting.

Allowing her only a moment to stretch out the first climax, he rolled them over and repositioned them on the big bed. She was under him—a place he'd wanted her since he'd first seen her. And now, here she was. Ready. Primed. His cock already deep inside her. A dream come true.

Steve began to move, watching her responses for the minutest change. Within moments, she was with him again, her body straining under his, her breath hitching in time with his thrusts.

"More!" she cried out as he ratcheted up the tempo, straining toward release. It would be a big one this time, taking them both to the stars and beyond. He just knew it.

Steve reached between them and played with her clit, holding her gaze as her eyes glazed with passion. He breathing was fast and harsh in the quiet of the room, as was his. Never before had a woman driven him to such heights, and Steve knew his life would be different from here on out. He had a mate now. Sex would never be the same. It would be better.

He increased his pace, something primitive driving him to claim, to possess. Trisha didn't seem to mind as she made his name into a litany of passion that drove him higher, harder, faster.

Until the tension burst in a blinding flash of rapture that made him groan even as she screamed his name, her body convulsing in pleasure around his, drawing out his climax.

They shot to the stars together, dancing among them for long, long minutes of the most intense sexual satisfaction he had ever known.

*Damn.* It was even better than he'd imagined. Having a mate. Fucking her brains out. Wanting to do it all again. Always. With love. And respect.

Having a mate was a magical thing and the fact that his mate was Trisha was the most magical thing of all. His heart expanded and he wasn't surprised to know she now lived within it for all time. As far as he was concerned, Trisha was it for him. He'd never love another.

A phone call woke Steve early the next morning. It was so early, in fact, that the sun wasn't really up. He fumbled around for the cell phone he'd left on the night stand, finally snagging it on the second or third try. He wasn't normally so uncoordinated, but a certain little water sprite had taken most of his energy, he thought with an inward grin.

He looked over at her sleeping next to him. The phone hadn't disturbed her slumber and he was glad. She needed her rest after everything she'd been through in the previous twenty-four hours. Steve could use a little more sleep, but cats were mostly nocturnal anyway. And shifters didn't need much shut-eye compared to their human counterparts, so he was alert and awake enough to deal with whatever the ringing phone at oh-dark-thirty meant.

He rolled out of the bed and padded barefoot across the carpet. He didn't want to disturb Trisha if he could help it. He went into the hallway and pushed the door to the bedroom until it was only open about an inch—through which he could clearly see his sleeping mate still snuggled in his bed.

"What?" he finally answered the phone with only a bit of impatience. Being with his mate had definitely already mellowed him a bit.

"I just got a call from Tony." Grif's voice came through the earpiece of the phone clearly. An early morning call from the local Master vampire couldn't be good news. "Somebody staked Jorge a few hours ago. Tony had already heard about your run-in with Jorge last night, and wanted to know what he'd done to earn a conversation from my second-in-command."

Steve trusted his older brother to know just how much information to give the bloodletter. The truce between *were* and vampire in this part of the country was a little stronger than in other places, but there still wasn't a lot of trust between the two supernatural races.

"Where?" Steve asked. He tried to keep his side of the conversation both low in volume and short in duration. He didn't want to wake up his mate if he had a choice.

"A few blocks down from the club. In an alley," Grif reported. "Nobody would've known but for a minion of Tony's who'd been following Jorge on Tony's orders. He wasn't kidding when he said he was taking care of the situation. The last time I talked to him was to lodge a formal complaint about Jorge harassing some of the young female wolves. He propositioned them, hoping one would be foolish enough to agree to let him drink from her. Shifter blood is like a drug to vamps. I think Jorge was looking for a fix, and I warned Tony about the potential problem. No way was I going to let that bloodsucker prey on our people."

Steve had known about the incident with the young wolves, but he hadn't been privy to the details of the conversation between the two leaders until now. He was glad to know that Tony had taken Grif's words seriously enough to have his own man watched. Such actions boded well for the ongoing relationship between Las Vegas's shifter and vamp populations.

"The tail didn't see who got Jorge?" Steve asked in low tones.

"Got there too late. Whoever did it was fast and silent. Which I think is why Tony called. He probably half-suspected you, or one of our other Clansmen seen at the bar, had done it. I assured him that all our people's movements were accounted for. To convince him, I had to tell him about the humans being drugged."

"What was his reaction?" Sometimes a lot could be gleaned from what the vampire *didn't* say, Steve knew. He'd had his share of dealings with Tony since moving to Las Vegas.

"That's why I'm calling. He said he's seen something like what I described before. Apparently one of the younger vamps was given wine laced with something similar two weeks ago. She got very sick from it and only just recovered a couple of days ago. Tony questioned her and discovered she'd been approached a few days before she fell ill, by a warlock who knew exactly what she was and wanted to know more about her magical abilities. She didn't tell him much, but they flirted. Apparently, the warlock appealed to her and she considered drinking from him but decided against it after their conversation turned odd and began to make her suspicious."

"Did he get a description?"

"Yeah. She drew him. Luckily, she's something of an artist. I already have a copy of the sketch and I just emailed it to you. Take a look. I'll wait."

Steve turned his smart phone over and brought up the image on the tiny screen. It was enough. He cursed under his breath as his jaw tightened. He held the phone back to his ear to tell Grif what he knew.

"I've seen him before. Last night, at the bar, he was definitely there, but he didn't approach the women, so I thought nothing of it until just now. And I saw the same guy on our surveillance footage of the incident a few weeks ago with the raptor girls. Remember Joseline and Fedora reported being followed by something that gave them the creeps, but they couldn't see? They were able to shift and fly away. I got footage of the area—one of the casino security officers owed me a favor—and I studied all the faces, but I couldn't tell from the tape who it was that menaced the girls," Steve reminded his brother. "This guy, though, he was on the tape."

"And in the bar," Grif repeated, accusation clear in his tone.

"Yeah," Steve agreed. "We need to find out who he is and why he's preying on magical young women."

"Well, we already know one thing. He's a warlock. The vamps have given us that much. And Tony's already got his people working on finding the guy. He said he'd work with us on this. Actually, he wanted our help in tracking the warlock down. I agreed. I'm even gladder I did now after what you've just told me."

"Yeah," Steve repeated. "I'll forward the image to everyone on my teams, but I think we need to go one step further and circulate the sketch to everyone in the Clan—especially the young females."

"Agreed. I'll issue the warning and sketch. You handle the security teams." Grif paused slightly. "How are things with your lady? Is she feeling all right after all the excitement?"

"She's resilient," Steve was proud to say, though he didn't want to go into details—not even with his brother. The relationship was too new. Too precious to him. Steve didn't really want to discuss his mate with anyone just yet. "She'll be okay. She's sleeping now, but I'm sure as soon as she wakes she's going to want to go check on her friends."

"They're doing fine. Sleeping it off. I've been getting regular updates from Kate. She's watching over them like a mother hen."

"Have you slept at all?" Steve was concerned for his brother. The Alpha was, by nature, the strongest of them all, but even he needed to sleep sometimes.

"Cat naps," Grif chuckled. "It's enough for now. I already promised my mate a weekend at the lake when this is over. She and I both need a little break from Clan life and some time alone."

It was odd for an Alpha werecat to have amassed such a large family of shifters around himself, but Grif had done it. Cats liked to roam and be by themselves sometimes, but the

Redstone brothers had managed to keep the larger Clan together by taking turns and filling in for each other when they felt the need to let their wildcat run free.

"That sounds nice. We'll cover for you, as usual," Steve said automatically.

Grif chuckled on the other end of the line. "Thanks for the offer, but I'm pretty sure you'll be heading for the hills with your mate too, once she's out of danger. One of the others will cover for us both."

Steve liked the sound of that. A weekend—or however long he could manage—alone somewhere peaceful with his mate. Yeah, big brother knew what he was talking about. The more Steve thought about it, the more he realized Grif was right. As soon as this situation was resolved, he was going to take Trisha somewhere. Just the two of them. Alone. Together.

It already sounded like paradise.

"Yeah, you got me there," Steve admitted. "It's still kind of new to be thinking in terms of having a mate."

"You get used to it," Grif commiserated. "In fact, you'll begin to wonder how you ever handled anything alone, once you realize how much help a mate can be."

"I look forward to it," Steve said with a grin. It was a nice thing to think about—not being alone anymore. Oh, he'd had his family, but cats liked to go their own way and have their own space.

Not anymore. Now all Steve could think about was sharing each moment, each day, each breath, with Trisha.

They ended the call shortly thereafter, each off to do the tasks they'd discussed. Steve was able to send out the image and the alert to everyone on his team using just his phone. The Clan had gone hi-tech years ago and kept pace with every advancement in electronics and communication. It was a hobby of Steve's, in particular. He had a little workshop in the basement filled with all sorts of toys and doo-dads, and he spent time tinkering down there whenever he had a chance.

As he finished up sending the message, the bedroom door opened. Trisha was standing there wrapped in a sheet, sleepy eyed and deliciously rumpled.

"What time is it?" She rubbed her eyes and then pushed her hair back from her face with one hand, holding onto the sheet with the other.

"Almost dawn."

"Why are you standing out here playing with your phone? Someone call?"

"Yeah, my brother Grif had some news. The vampire who tried to seduce you and your friends last night was killed shortly thereafter."

"Wait. There was a vampire? Are those things even real?" She shook her head. "Of course they are. You're real. And so am I. Darnit all. Somebody died last night?" She looked a little unsteady on her feet and almost adorably confused, but not knowing basic stuff about their world could be very dangerous. He had a great deal to tell her about.

"Why don't we go downstairs and I can make some coffee or something. There's a lot to discuss."

What followed was an hour of talking, seated at his kitchen table while she learned the ins and outs of the supernatural world. When they got down to the specifics of what had happened to Jorge, he discovered her compassionate nature, which didn't really surprise him at all.

"I hate to think this Jorge guy was killed just because he approached us. That seems a bit extreme." She sipped at the tall glass of water she'd refilled twice already. She certainly seemed to thrive on the stuff.

"He wasn't a good guy. He's been warned before about his bad behavior and that's why the Master vamp of the area had him followed. That turned out good for us because now we know we can eliminate him as a suspect in this situation *and*—" he emphasized the word as he refilled his glass with orange juice, "—I don't have to worry about him harassing anyone ever again. Or worse."

"Was he really that bad?"

"The Master thought enough about our complaints to have him watched. That says something. Tony wouldn't have acted on our words alone, I don't think. He probably had his own feelings on the matter. Vamps don't really move around a lot. They settle in a place for fifty years or more, usually. So the fact that Jorge had relocated several times in the past few years didn't bode well for him from the start."

She drained her glass and stood to refill it. "You have a filtration system on this tap, right?" she asked as she filled the glass at his kitchen sink.

"Installed it myself," he answered with some satisfaction. "*Weres* have sensitive taste buds as well as noses. Most of us filter out the chemicals the municipal water supply adds to our homes. Or we drill our own wells, but that can be problematic too, depending on what part of the country we're in. Not all groundwater is clean."

"Yeah, I know. That's one of the things I can do," she admitted with seeming shyness. Steve was intrigued.

"You can purify water?" he asked carefully, not wanting to seem too eager with his questioning. She would tell him what she wanted him to know. He just had to be patient.

"I can call springs. I sense water. I know where it is and if it's clean or not. If it's not, I can make it flow places that will clean it—through limestone deposits or sand or whatnot. For instance, I know where the water lies deep underground here. It's very far down, but there's a surprising amount of it for the climate. I wouldn't have expected so much hiding under a desert.

"Really?" Steve was impressed. He tried not to make a big deal out of her words, hoping she'd open up more.

"I can also call rain from the sky. If there are clouds, I can coax them into releasing their bounty."

"I bet you really enjoy the ocean, huh?" He almost didn't want to hear her answer because he lived in a desert.

If he had to move to the coast to make his mate happy, he'd do it, but he'd really miss his family and he didn't want to let them down. He was second-in-command here. If he left, it would leave the Clan diminished. His other brothers would have to step up and most of them were off on their own at the moment, being tomcats. He understood and he wanted to give his younger brothers their time to roam, but his mate's happiness had to come first.

"Actually, the ocean is a little...overwhelming is the word, I guess. Dad says you get used to it, but I never really have."

"Is it the salt water? I thought you liked my pool out back." Steve was trying his best to understand her, but her abilities were like nothing he'd ever imagined.

"No, I really like salt water. It's softer on my skin and more buoyant. But the ocean is full of life. Life like you can't even imagine. And I can sense it all. I can talk to some of them too. Dolphins have really good senses of humor. Whales are more grown-up, except for some of the smaller species. And some of those turtles can be downright depressing. They don't see the world the way we do. It's interesting, but it's a lot to take in."

"Are you sure you aren't a mermaid?" He sent her a smile, hoping his casual attitude and humor would put her even more at ease. He liked that she was opening up to him. He sensed this wasn't stuff she talked about with just anyone.

"Nah." She smiled and wiggled the toes on one foot. "No tail, see?" Then she sobered. "They're not real too, are they?"

Steve had to laugh. "You'd know better than I, sweetheart. I don't spend a lot of time in the ocean, though I do love the water." He drank the last of his juice and put the glass in the sink. "Selkies now, they are real. Your dad might know some of them. A few of them are Navy SEALs. I think they like the irony."

Trisha laughed and the sound enchanted him. "Selkies are men that turn into seals, right? I think I read a book about Ireland once that mentioned the myth."

"More than myth," Steve confirmed. "Those dudes are badass. But they don't hide their skins like in the old legends. That's all bunk. They're shifters, just like the rest of us." He reconsidered his words and added a caveat. "Well, maybe they have a little more magic than most."

"Dad never called what we do magic. It sounds like a parlor trick when you use that word, even though I know you're serious." She tilted her head and looked kind of adorably embarrassed. "I don't mean to belittle your beliefs. This is all just a little hard to get used to. I was raised thinking I was a lone freak in a world of mostly normal people.

"First of all, you're not a freak. You are a wonderfully magical woman with an affinity for water. And if you exist, why didn't you think others like you, but with different abilities, could exist? And I didn't take offense, by the way. I know this is all new to you."

"Dad always said we were the only ones. He never entertained my fantasies about magic and wizards and such when I was a girl. He pretty much outlawed that kind of stuff in our house. Ask Deke."

Steve frowned and then sighed. "You know we're going to have to come clean with him sooner or later. Trisha…" He hesitated, not knowing how to phrase what he wanted to say and worried that it was too soon to talk of the future. But the cat inside him clawed at him to speak the words of claim. He'd obey the cat—to a point. "I feel things for you," he said, not sure where to go from there. He tried again. "Shifters usually know right away when they've met someone special." He ran his hand through his hair in frustration. This wasn't coming out right at all. "Trish, what I'm trying to say is that I think you're special. To me. Special to me. And that what we've started here is just that. A start. It's not a fling or a casual anything. It's serious. Something I treasure and want to continue."

He rested his hand on the table and she reached out and covered it with one of her own. Her fingers were so small and delicate compared to his. Everything about her enchanted him. Especially her smile as she met his gaze. It gave him hope.

"I'm really glad you said that, because I'm feeling things for you that I've never felt for anyone else. Strange things.

Magical things—in the best possible sense of the word. It's like we were meant to make love and be friends."

"I want to be more than friends, Trisha." He couldn't help the way his voice dropped into the rumble range. It was the cat purring inside him at the female's positive response.

"I think I want that too. I don't understand it, and I've never had this kind of reaction to anyone before in my life, but I'd really like to see where it goes—if you're feeling the same way, that is."

Her uncertainty almost made him laugh, but he wouldn't embarrass her like that. He didn't want her to misunderstand his reactions. Not now. Not at such an important juncture.

He set his chair back from the table and took her hand, coaxing her to stand and come over to him and then sit on his lap. She followed where he led until she was ensconced in his arms, her luscious thighs spread as she straddled him. He claimed her mouth gently, rubbing their bodies together. It was a tender kiss. A kiss of gentle possession that spoke of his desire and respect for her.

"I definitely feel the same way," he murmured against her lips when he finally let them both come up for air. "I have never felt the mating urge before, but it hit me the moment your real scent hit me."

"Scent, huh? When was this?" She drew a few inches away to look into his eyes, one of her delicate eyebrows raised in skepticism.

"After you took that shower at the Pack house. Before that, the chemical was fouling your scent. When you scrubbed it away and your real scent was revealed, well, my knees went weak. I knew then that you were special. Trisha, I think you're my mate."

There it was. His heart on a platter, if she only recognized it.

"Mate, huh? That means something special among your people, doesn't it?" Her expression was very serious and somewhat closed to him, which made him uncomfortable. He hoped he hadn't said too much.

"It's very special. As special as you are," he answered obliquely, kissing her nose and setting her away.

She cooperated, standing when he did, though he would've given anything to keep her on his lap and maybe have some kitchen sex to start their day. But the conversation had gotten out of his control and he panicked. Time to change the subject. He needed something to throw her off the trail.

"Do you want to call Deke or shall I?"

Yeah, that did the trick. Her expression went from speculative to frowning in the blink of an eye. She didn't want to call her brother. That much was obvious. But Steve knew the longer they put it off, the angrier Deke would be. Better to deal with him now, while the situation was still salvageable. Somewhat.

"I guess I'd better. I don't want to, you understand." She pointed her finger at him, which he thought was cute. "I'll take a shower, dress and then we can call him together. I'll want you nearby for him to yell at when he starts to boil over. Deal?"

Steve nodded, smiling. She knew her brother well. "It's the least I can do."

# CHAPTER SEVEN

Trisha was confused by Steve's sudden retreat, but she liked what he'd been saying. She thought about their conversation as she tidied up in his shower. He really had a gorgeous house. The shower stall was huge. Tiled in earthy, light-colored stone with a bench and little shelves located out of the direct spray of water. They held bottles of herbal shampoo and soap. It was his shampoo. The scent was subtle. Nothing flowery or feminine about this master suite at all.

She took it as a good sign. If he was in the habit of entertaining female overnight guests in his home, surely there would be some sign of it in the bathroom at least. She'd already looked in the closet and drawers, but only his clothes were in there. She didn't feel guilty about her snooping. She wanted this guy in her life on a long-term basis. She had a right to check him out. Or so her overprotective brother and father had always taught her. Go into a situation with your eyes open and you won't be surprised later when things happen.

Only she hadn't been prepared for repeated attacks on what was supposed to be a quick jaunt to Vegas for a bachelorette party. What had she missed? Or was there any way she could have known this would happen in the first place? Probably not. Heck, she hadn't even known magical creatures like *weres* and warlocks and such existed.

In retrospect, it seemed kind of stupid of her not to question her father's adamant refusal to acknowledge magic in any form. He never called what they could do *magic*. He just said they had special gifts and that they were the only ones. She thought now he must have been lying.

That was not an accusation she would make lightly. Not even in the privacy of her own mind. One did not simply call Admiral Morrow a liar.

Trisha finished with her shower quickly. No lazing around in the water, putting off the hard task of calling her family. They needed to know something was wrong. In fact, she was surprised either Deke or her dad hadn't called already. Those guys had a spooky sixth sense about trouble.

She dressed in one of the casual outfits she'd packed. She was grateful to Steve and his unseen minions who had retrieved her suitcase from the hotel. It was nice to have her own things, and if she was going to stay here much longer, she'd clutter up that pretty master bath with her toiletries. As it was, for now, she was just glad to have clean clothes.

She picked up her cell phone and went downstairs, checking the email and messages as she went, wondering why her family hadn't already been in touch. She needed to call them...

And then she realized she wouldn't need to make that call after all.

She heard voices from the living room and knew them both very well indeed. Trisha walked quietly over to the archway that led to the spacious living room and leaned against the frame.

"Hi, Dad."

Three sets of masculine eyes turned to look at her. Steve was standing by the cold fireplace while Deke had taken up a position to one side and the admiral had faced Steve straight on. Neither of the Morrow men looked happy. In fact, she could tell they were both pissed off. Royally pissed off. At her. At Steve. It didn't matter when they were in this mood.

Everyone in the vicinity was fair game.

"Patricia Anne Morrow, why in the world haven't you been in touch?"

Uh-oh. The full name. Yeah, her dad was really mad. He only pulled out the full name for special occasions. And they weren't the good kind of occasions.

"I was going to call you this morning. I just wanted to take a shower first and get dressed. Then I was going to call. I swear." She held up the phone, still in her hand. Her father seemed unimpressed.

"I thought you were a better man than this, Redstone." The admiral turned his condemnation on Steve. "You should have called Derek the moment she got into trouble."

"And just how was he going to explain to Deke—my human half-brother—that a Pack of werewolves helped me escape a magical attack? His hands were tied by the need for secrecy among his kind."

"The attack was magical?"

Thank goodness, she'd managed to deflect a bit of her father's anger onto the actual problem at hand. She knew he wouldn't let it go completely, but he was more of a bottom-line kind of guy. He'd want to know exactly what they were up against and how to counteract it first, before he let loose his fury on all and sundry.

"I believe the drug they used was both mundane and magical," she declared. "It had a strong anesthetic that had some kind of silver catalyst. And Steve's friends swear it had a magical component."

"What friends?" Her father's clipped words were aimed at Steve.

"Do you know a covert operative named Slade?" Steve paused until her father nodded. "He's recently joined our Clan. His mate is a priestess of the Lady. They both have high-level magical skills. They can *see* magic. And they said it was all over the women we brought to the Pack house."

"But the silver made you sick, right?" her dad asked quickly, as if he already knew the answer.

"Me and Lynda. We both tossed our cookies and are both awake now. The rest are still asleep and will be for a while."

"Lynda?" Deke spoke for the first time, his voice raised in question.

"She's half-fey," Steve answered off-handedly.

That was news to Trisha. "Fey? Like a fairy? They're real too?" She shot a look full of accusation at her father when Steve nodded. "Why did you lie to me all these years? Why didn't you tell me there were other beings out there with gifts? People who could shapeshift. Vampires. And now fairies. Darnit! I've been friends with her for years!" Trisha was feeling angry herself now. "Why couldn't you be straight with me?"

"It was for your own protection."

The answer was lame and she judged by her father's expression that he realized it.

"Maybe when I was a kid, but I'm an adult now, Dad. I can handle the truth. You shouldn't have kept me in the dark. Maybe then, I would've been better prepared for this. And maybe—just maybe—it wouldn't have happened."

She crossed her arms and dropped into one of the cushy chairs in the room. She wasn't happy about being lied to by omission and it was important that her father knew it. Judging by the expression on his face and the set of his shoulders, he was getting the message. Good.

Silence reigned for a moment until Deke finally spoke. "So you're a werewolf, huh?" he asked Steve.

"No. Cougar. Werecougar," Steve corrected him.

"Then how did the wolves become involved?" her father wanted to know, back to business for the moment.

"As I was trying to explain…" Steve shot her a glance and she knew she'd interrupted him in the middle of the story. "My brother is the Alpha of the Redstone Clan. The base of our Clan is and always has been cougar. But we expanded years ago to include everyone who works for us. We have a few wolf Packs, raptor Tribes of various kinds, other cats too. Pretty much anyone who works for our company and wants to come under Grif's authority. Being part of our Clan has its advantages and quite a few smaller Packs, Clans and Tribes have joined us over the years. They each have their own Alphas and organizational structures, depending on what animal they share their souls with, but ultimately, they come under Grif as the overall Alpha. I'm his second-in-command and head of security."

Both Deke and her dad seemed impressed in a guarded sort of way. Trisha was proud of Steve and his family, even though she didn't really understand the full extent of their reach. She knew Redstone Construction was a huge company that did projects all over the country. If all those people were shifters and they followed Grif, then he and his family had to have a lot of power indeed. She was impressed too, when she thought about it.

"I was watching Trisha's group when a bloodletter approached them. I knew he'd been in trouble before, so I motioned him over to warn him off. While we were talking, a few of our wolves moved in on the ladies. It turned out to be a good thing because when the fight started—which I believe was a deliberate attempt to drive the girls out into a waiting ambush—the wolves were there to protect them. They called for help at my signal, and being wolves, they called their Packmates. The ambush was foiled and we took the girls, who were starting to get woozy by then, to the Pack house. We had to stop on the way for Trisha and Lynda to ralf on a few cactuses, and by the time we arrived all the others were unconscious."

"I checked them over with Kate's help. We took blood samples and I used the Redstone lab to discover what the compound was. Kate and Lynda have been keeping an eye on the girls while I recovered from the second ambush."

"Second ambush?" Deke looked angry again. Trisha sighed and passed the verbal baton back over to Steve. He seemed better at explaining things in a way that didn't make her male family members mad.

"We were on our way back to the Pack house from the lab

when a truck totaled my SUV. Trisha took a bad hit to the leg, but when I realized water was her element, I rerouted here so we could use my pool out back. She healed up and slept it off."

"In your bed," Deke accused with a sneer.

Trisha wasn't taking any of that. No way. No how. She stood and marched over to her brother.

"Where I sleep and who I sleep with are none of your damn business!"

"You slept with him?" Deke's voice thundered through the room.

And then silence.

"There's something else you need to know," Steve said in a soft voice. He stood straighter, squaring his broad shoulders before declaring, "Trisha is my mate."

For the first time in her life, Trisha saw the admiral falter. He almost collapsed onto the sofa behind him, as if needing the support, and his face was ashen.

"Mate?" Deke asked, clearly confused. "Is that like your girlfriend or something?"

"No, Deke," Steve answered in a calm, sober voice. "Among shifters, mating is for life."

Now it was Trisha who needed the support of a chair. She settled for leaning against the back of the nearest one, her knees wobbling a bit.

"Wait a minute." Deke seemed to need clarification. "Are you saying you want to *marry* my sister?"

Trisha held her breath as she turned to look at Steve. Her heart was crying out *yes, yes, yes!* But her head was confused by the speed at which this was all happening.

"Among my kind, simply declaring myself means she's off-limits to others. If she accepts my claim, then in the eyes of my people we're already married. But if she wants a fancy human ceremony…" Steve turned to her, holding her gaze, his words very solemn and serious. "I'll give her anything she desires. For the rest of our lives. And beyond."

Silence held for a moment and then everything happened

at once. Trisha began to move toward Steve, but her father stood abruptly and came between them. Blocked. But maybe it was for the best?

"Look, she doesn't have to decide anything right away. She doesn't *have to* accept, right?" Deke asked.

"She could decline," Steve admitted, and Trisha sensed there was more to it than just saying no.

What would happen to him if she refused him? It didn't sound like he could just pick any woman to mate with. He'd made it sound a lot more serious than that. She chewed her lip, worrying over what she didn't know.

But her father was clearly not going to let her find out the answers to her many questions now. No, he was buying time. He probably was planning an offensive to get her to refuse. To be brutally honest, she didn't know what she wanted. Her heart wanted Steve. That much was clear. Her mind, however, was still struggling with everything she'd learned in such a short span of time.

It was a lot to take in.

So she let her dad come between them. She let him buy her time to figure things out. She didn't like hurting Steve with her uncertainty, but she needed this time. Desperately. She was so confused by everything.

Just then, the doorbell rang. The tension in the room deflated as Steve turned to go answer it, leaving her alone with her brother and father.

Much to her surprise, the moment they were alone, her father turned to her. Instead of ripping her a new one, he gathered her into his arms and just hugged her, squeezing her tight. She realized then how worried he'd been.

"I'm sorry, Daddy. I thought we could fix this and then tell you about it all later, when everything was safe again." She whispered her words against his chest but knew he could hear.

After a moment, he let her go. "You might've gotten away with it, but not with Deke's special radar. He always knows when something's wrong. You should've known he would sense the trouble you're in." Her dad smiled and passed her off to Deke, who gathered her into a second big hug.

"How could you lie to me on the phone? And how did you get Red to lie?" He let her go and moved back, a funny expression coming over his face. "Forget I asked. I know why he lied. He'd do anything for you. That much is clear, though I never thought you could actually leash a cat."

"On the contrary," a new voice came into the room. It was Slade, followed closely by Grif and another man who looked so much like Grif and Steve that he had to be another of their brothers. "Cats can be quite biddable under the right circumstances." Slade smiled as he finished his thought, walking over to shake hands with her father first and then exchange a backslapping handshake with her brother. He clearly knew them both.

He stepped back and Grif made a similar greeting and then introduced his brother. "This is Mag. He's been liaising with the bloodletters for us."

"And letting them nibble a bit too, it appears," her father said as he shook Mag's hand, tugging him to the side so he could look at the bite marks that were fading on his neck. "Voluntarily?"

Mag nodded. "She's an old friend who was held prisoner for a long time. She's very weak. She needs the boost my blood gives her."

"Just be careful not to give her too much," her father cautioned. "Vampires are unpredictable creatures at the best of times."

He let Mag go so he could shake hands with Deke and then they all sat down and got comfortable. Trisha decided to sit with Steve and he made room for her on the settee. Her father and brother frowned at her, but she didn't care. She needed the reassurance of having Steve near her in this gathering.

Funny. She would have turned to her dad once upon a time, but since meeting Steve, it seemed natural to seek support from him. She'd have to examine that reaction in detail later. It definitely meant something, but there was too much going on to analyze it now.

"It's good to finally be able to come clean with you both," Grif started the conversation. "If we'd known you came from a magical family, Deke, we could've been more open before when we were all working together."

"It's okay," Deke said offhandedly. "I was raised to understand the need for secrecy. I respected your right to keep your own secrets, though I always did privately wonder what you guys were."

They went over everything that had happened last night again, with the added benefit of what Slade and Grif's other people had been able to learn, plus the vampire perspective that Mag reported. Apparently, all the vampires were up in arms because one of their number had been staked by someone outside their community. It wasn't a common occurrence and they were worried there might be a vampire hunter on the loose, which apparently happened from time to time.

So the vamps were all out searching by night for clues. They'd even reached out to Grif to share information and have the *weres* continue the search by day. By pooling their information, they were coming up with a more complete picture of what was going on.

"The warlock's name is Jeffrey Billings," Slade summed up the information they'd gathered. "He's a low-level magic user, but he seems to have one special talent. He's a sensitive. He probably picked up on the magic around the girls—either from you, Trisha, or your half-fey friend—and he probably wants it for himself. We've seen a rise in magic users of evil intent trying to steal power from Others."

"How do you come by this intel?" the admiral wanted to know.

Grif answered. "The Lords of all *Were* have been keeping track of incidents and reporting down through the Alphas ever since their mate was attacked. It seems the *Venifucus* are back and some are even talking about restoring Elspeth to power."

"Elspeth? *Venifucus?*" Deke repeated while their father just looked grim. Apparently there were some things the admiral hadn't shared with Deke.

"Elspeth was known as the Destroyer of Worlds," Trisha's dad surprised her by saying. The old man knew a lot more than he'd ever told her—or Deke, for that matter. "She was fey—or at least part-fey. She had incredible magical power according to my father, who fought in many battles against her minions—the secret society called the *Venifucus*. When she was banished to the farthest realm, they were thought to be defeated. Most of them died trying to save her, but my father always suspected a few survived, though he probably never anticipated they would return as a viable group."

"Why isn't she dead? How could she still be around?" Trisha asked, puzzled and trying to add up the years in her mind. It just didn't compute.

"Fey don't die," he answered, shocking her. "Or at least, they live so long as to seem immortal and don't succumb to ordinary illnesses. They can be killed only under special circumstances. Silver, of course, is as poisonous to them as it is to the rest of us magical folk. But Elspeth had more magic than most. More than even the greatest mages of the time. More than all those who were arrayed against her could claim. And it was thought that to simply kill her—if it could be done at all—would be too easy a punishment. The many beings she'd wronged wanted her to suffer as their families had suffered. They wanted her to understand pain and sorrow. They also wanted to end her without losing even more lives. The easiest way—and believe me, from what my father said, it was by no means *easy*—was to amass enough magic and strike at just the right time and place to send her through a portal to one of the many forgotten realms, where she could suffer her eternity alone, contemplating all the misery she'd caused here on earth."

Silence reigned in the room until finally Slade cleared his throat.

"Forgive me, Admiral. I've never had the chance to speak with anyone who actually knew someone who'd fought in the war against the *Venifucus*. Few species are long-lived enough. You must be several hundred years old, if you don't mind the observation."

"Seven hundred and fifty-two, actually. I waited a long time to find my true mate and start a family." He actually smiled at Trisha and she realized her mouth was gaping open in shock.

She looked around the room and everyone seemed to be taking his news in stride. They believed him and didn't blink an eye at the idea that he was way older than any normal person had a right to be. She'd thought he was fifty-two, not *seven hundred* and fifty-two. This was going to take some getting used to.

"Then the magic runs strong in your species," Grif observed, nodding toward Trisha. "That's both good and bad. Given a chance to grow old gracefully, cougars can last several centuries. Sadly, our ancestors often lived very chaotic lives and few got the chance to do so. I like to think that by banding together as we have in the Redstone Clan and under the guidance of the Lords, our current generations will have a much better shot at living to ripe old ages without the internal conflicts and fights for dominance."

*Whoa.* Now not only was her dad hundreds of years older than she thought, but they were saying that Steve and his brothers would live just as long? And what about her? The mind-boggling thought that if her dad had been around so long, she probably would be too… It was almost too much to process.

Steve took her hand and squeezed it, grounding her. She looked at him and realized he could be way older than she thought he was. That was something she'd have to ask him about privately. She didn't want to draw any more attention to their personal situation at the moment. Not while she had her father so neatly distracted from his initial anger.

"I'm glad you strive for peace. I have known shapeshifters

in my time who were not quite so noble," her father answered with a hint of steel in his gaze. She knew that look. He wasn't happy she was mixed up with a cougar. "Tell me more about this Billings," he ordered, back on target for the problem at hand. Trisha almost breathed a sigh of relief, but she knew better than that.

She didn't think for one minute that he'd forgotten about the other little problem—the fact that Steve said she was his mate. But she knew her father's methodic nature. She knew he'd eliminate the most immediate threat first, then work his way down his priority list. She only hoped that by the time they came back to her relationship with Steve, she'd know what to do about it herself.

Slade continued his briefing. "We know Billings has preyed on magical women before—with no success that we are aware of. It could be he's looking to make a score but hasn't managed it yet, although he's upped his game since the earlier attempts with the female bloodletter and the werewolf girls. He's never been so organized before. Never had help that we know of. Never tried ambushes. The previous encounters were clumsy head-on affairs that lacked the organization of what occurred last night."

"So either he's perfecting his plan of attack or—" Steve began.

"He now has help," her father finished the thought. "Dammit. I was hoping we were wrong."

The admiral and Deke shared a speaking glance that Trisha recognized. "Spill, you two. What do you know?"

"Nothing concrete," Deke said first. "I only told Dad what I sensed. Something very wrong here. A threat against you from something very dark. He did the rest."

"I called on the water. It can sometimes show me what it's witnessed. There's not a lot around here to work with—though the casinos have a surprising number of water features, I was pleased to discover. Deke and I didn't come straight here. We knew you were safe with Steve, so we did some recon on the Strip. The water says you were followed by more than one man. I was hoping it was wrong, because it was vague. There are so many people walking around down there. But in light of the intel, I'm giving my initial information more credence. There are at least two people in on this. One is the weaker—probably the warlock we know about. But there is a stronger one. A puppet master, perhaps, pulling the strings and organizing the escalated action. The stronger one has the resources the weaker one lacks, but not the sensitivity to know who to target."

"That makes almost too much sense," Grif muttered. "That means potentially everyone with magic around them— all my Clansmen and our Other friends—could be at risk here if the sensitive latches onto their trail."

Her father nodded, his expression grim.

"There's only one thing to do then." Grif stood. "We need to bait the trap and catch them before they can succeed in actually capturing anyone." He whipped out his phone and began to dial, but the admiral stood and drew his attention.

"Warn your Clan to stand clear, Alpha. My daughter started this. I will end it." He spoke in that determined voice that made him such a great leader of men. When his blue gaze turned to her, Trisha was surprised. "With Trisha's help," he added, completely flooring her. She'd fully expected him to lock her in a basement where she couldn't possibly be in danger. Instead, he seemed to want her in on the action. For once. Wow.

Steve squeezed her hand and his jaw clenched. "I don't like that idea."

"Neither do I, frankly, but I think we have to do it this way. The warlock is already locked on to her for whatever reason. She's not unskilled, just unaware of the presence of Others. I'm sorry, honey, I thought it was best to keep you innocent of the magic all around you. Some of it isn't very nice. If it's any consolation, I would've told you eventually. All this has just shown me I put it off too long."

As apologies went, it was better than most. She thought she understood what motivated her dad. He'd always been the one to protect her and his devotion to keeping her and her mother safe from all harm and worry was shared by Deke. Her brother might not be genetically related to the old man, but they were cut from the same cloth. Between the two of them, she and her mom hadn't had to worry about their personal safety, or much of anything else—except the exceptionally dangerous line of work both men had chosen to pursue.

"It's okay, Dad," she said softly, then squared her shoulders. "I'll do whatever I can to help end this threat. I don't like that my friends were hurt because of me."

"You might not have been the main target," Slade said from the other side of the room. "I talked with your friend Lynda at length. She could just as easily have been what drew the attention of the warlock. In fact, I wouldn't be surprised if she was the initial target. She stands out much more on the magical plane than you do, Trisha. Even your father has a deceptively low-grade magic around him right now. I imagine you both have some kind of natural shield unless you're actively using your abilities. The use of your magic last night lit the sky with its incandescence, but today it's muted again, like the admiral's." Slade sent an almost apologetic look toward her dad. "But your half-fey friend has no skill at dampening her magical output. She shines to my sight."

"Then why did they go after me again last night on the way back from the lab?" she wanted to know.

"Target of opportunity," Steve answered from between tightly drawn lips. He wasn't happy about any of this, she could tell. "The fey was locked up in the Pack house with the other girls, surrounded by wolves and firmly in their territory. It would take an assault force bigger than the one that ambushed us to even begin to think about hitting the Pack house, but a small convoy was well within their abilities. Though they didn't count on us being shifters. They didn't have silver ammo and a few of them wet themselves when we went animal on them."

"Humans then. Possibly amateurs," Grif concluded.

"Hired guns who didn't know what they were going up against."

"Makes sense," the admiral acknowledged. "The next attempt will be more organized. That's the pattern so far. Each attack gets a little more sophisticated. They're learning as they go."

"It won't be fast enough," Grif spoke the words like a vow. "We have more than cats and dogs to count on. I can get aerial support."

"Planes? Helos?" Deke asked.

Grif smiled. "Raptors. Shapeshifters who transform into eagles and hawks."

Trisha noted the way her brother's eyes widened.

"Impressive," was all Deke said. He was playing it cool, but Trisha knew her brother had to be really impressed to say even that much.

"And Kate and I will provide magical support, if needed," Slade put in.

"The vamps are gathering and will help if this goes down at night," Magnus reported.

Trisha tried to relax as the men began to make plans and contingency plans. Her dad was in his element, strategizing on how best to deploy the troops. She just sat back and watched. So did Steve, much to her surprise. He leaned back in the chair and held her hand, simply watching the planning unfold. Occasionally, he'd add a comment or two, but mostly he held back and listened.

# CHAPTER EIGHT

"Tony's people are ready," Magnus reported, having just ended a phone call to his vampire connection.

Steve, Trisha, her dad and brother were pre-positioned in a hotel suite from where they would launch the evening's offensive. There was no guarantee they'd catch their fish tonight, but Trisha would give it her all. She wanted this over so she could get on with her life and end the threat against herself and her friends. Being ambushed every time she stepped out of the house wasn't her idea of fun.

But tonight they would welcome the attack. She *wanted* to draw the attention of the jerk who'd been trailing her. In fact, she'd left Steve's house earlier with a much heavier guard than the night before and they knew for a fact she was followed back to the hotel she'd been staying at before all this craziness started.

To the watchers, it probably seemed like she'd gone back to her hotel to get her stuff or something. They didn't attack the car Steve had dropped her off in and all the other guards were invisible to her eye, even though she knew they were there. Chances are, the enemy didn't know just how heavily guarded she'd been.

Steve had dropped her off in front of the hotel and she'd gone straight upstairs. All along the way, she'd been

113

conscious of the shapeshifters who kept a close watch on her path. The elevator had been filled with Redstones—Grif, Mag and another brother they called Bobcat. They'd escorted her not to her floor—though the elevator doors had opened dutifully at the floor where she'd originally been staying—but to the penthouse, where they'd reserved a spacious suite.

Steve was already there when she arrived. She didn't know how he'd gotten into position so quickly, but she was glad he was there.

The plan was simple. Trisha was going to leave the hotel and walk down the Strip. She wouldn't be alone, but it sure would *look* like she was alone. Her path would be monitored and guarded by shapeshifters stationed all around. And a group of vampires had agreed to steer traffic away from her—and whoever might follow her.

Apparently the vamps could alter people's perception and influence what they saw or even where they went. They'd be using their powers to isolate Trisha and the prey they were hoping to trap from the rest of the many tourists who roamed the Las Vegas Strip every night.

Trisha was going to walk toward the big hotel with a giant water feature out front. If things got too hairy for her, Trisha's safe haven was the water. She'd dive in and let the *weres* and vamps take care of the warlock. That was the plan. Only her father and she knew that as long as she was in or near a body of water, she could do more than any of the werepeople probably realized.

"It's show time," Steve whispered, standing opposite her, holding one of her hands. He moved closer and gave her a quick kiss, despite the frowns coming from her dad and brother's direction. "I'll be with you every step of the way, even if you can't see me. I can be there in a flash if you need me."

"Head for the water," her father reminded her as Steve stepped back. "You know what to do. The water will protect you."

"I know, Dad." She winked at him. It was a little knowing

gesture between them that spoke volumes about things only they shared.

He knew exactly what she was capable of—as she knew what he could do. Her dad was a formidable creature when his protective instincts were stirred. She'd seen it only a few times in her life and those times were more than memorable. If anything threatened his family or those under his protection, he could call on forces she wouldn't have believed if she hadn't seen it herself.

She had only a fraction of his power and even less of his experience, but she had practiced the things she could do, under his tutelage, all her life. They had a giant swimming pool at their house and they had made good use of it as a place to train her talents in secret. Deke had seen a good bit of what she could do, but even he didn't know the full extent of her abilities.

She only hoped she wouldn't have to use any of them. If the men were to be believed, the vampires would be screening them all from human observation while this went down, but she still felt really uncomfortable about using her talents where everyone could see. She'd been keeping the secret all her life and it was hard to let go of it now, all of a sudden. It was only yesterday that she'd learned there were other special creatures out there in the world.

Magic was real. That was something her father had never allowed her to know. She still felt a bit resentful at his deliberate attempts to keep her in ignorance. For now, she had to focus on the matter at hand. There was a threat to her and her friends and she was in the best position—with all this help—to end it. Finally, she'd get to put some of those protective instincts she'd been born with to good use.

Steve hated this plan. He hated sending Trisha out there into the unknown. Using her as bait. Everything about this went against his instincts, but from the moment her father had suggested it, a light had entered her eyes that he recognized. A light of battle. Of confidence. Of power.

It would crush her if he stepped in and argued against her participation. A predator to his very bones, he respected the right of every being to take an active part in their own protection. The fact that she was helping to safeguard her friends as well only amplified the need he knew she was feeling to do what she could.

If she'd been a shifter female, he would still have been concerned, but he would have had to respect her right to defend herself and those she considered friends. He had to give Trisha the same respect—even though he didn't really understand the full scope of her abilities.

But her father had to know. The admiral wasn't saying much, but the mere fact that he'd suggested this plan meant that he knew Trisha could handle it. Maybe he was making up, in some small way, for keeping her in the dark so long about the real world and her place in it—among magical beings, like herself.

If there was one thing that made Steve feel a little better about all of this, it was that the admiral had put forth the plan. Steve had worked with the man, and the SEALs under him many times in the past. He respected the admiral's head for strategy and his knowledge of the strengths and weaknesses of those under his command. He always deployed the best men for the job, and Steve saw no reason to doubt his judgment now, not when the man's own daughter was involved. *Especially* when his daughter was involved.

Admiral Morrow wouldn't risk his daughter's life on a mission she had a slim chance of seeing through to the end. Her father knew her abilities better than anyone. He had to believe she could handle her role in the coming action. And Steve had to believe that old man Morrow knew what he was doing when he selected his daughter for the mission.

Steve followed Trisha as she walked down the Las Vegas Strip. He was at quite a distance, using his keener eyesight and sense of smell to track her among the many humans all around. The vamps were doing their thing subtly. Their kind of magic was very low-key. In fact, if Steve didn't know they were out there, consciously working to direct the humans' attentions elsewhere, he wouldn't have known.

As it was, Steve could only see the small gestures, the quick aversion of eyes, the way nobody really looked at Trisha. Those small things told him the vamps were doing their thing. He'd given her an earwig—a tiny device that fit in her ear and would both transmit and receive audio signals. They—Steve, her father and brother—could hear her when she spoke and she could hear their directions as well.

She was on a separate frequency from the tactical radios the rest of the shifter team was using. Mag was their relay to the vamps. He was, at this moment, strolling down the Strip arm in arm with his vampire lady friend. Steve had met Miranda a couple of times—including the night they'd rescued her from a madman's lair. She'd been in bad shape. Her captor had starved her for months. Possibly years. Steve didn't really know. Mag had recognized her, let her bite the shit out of him in her frenzy and then disappeared with her into the night.

He'd taken her away from the scene so fast none of the brothers knew where he'd gone. He'd shown up a few days later, just long enough to get a couple of changes of clothes from his room and have angry words with Grif. Since then, he'd been around a little more often and he'd brought Miranda to a meeting on neutral territory so Grif could talk to them both. Steve hadn't been in on that meeting, but he knew Grif wouldn't have let Mag go if he thought the woman posed a real threat to either Mag or the Clan.

Steve could see Mag and Miranda walking along about a hundred yards from Trisha on the other side of the wide boulevard. Mag's arm was around Miranda's waist and it looked more like he was supporting her than anything else to Steve's keen eyes. Miranda was still sickly, which surprised him. Vamps were immortal. Very little could sicken them, though starvation had to be a bad thing. She must've suffered at the mad mage's hands more than Steve had realized. No wonder Mag was so secretive about the woman. The injured female must've roused all of his brother's protective instincts.

As Steve scanned the crowd, he could see the way the vamps orchestrated the zone of obscurity that moved along with Trisha. It was masterfully done and he would have never known of it if the vamps hadn't let him in on the magic. They were able to target exactly who could see the reality versus the rest of the world that saw the illusion they were creating. Only someone with very special, rare magical powers would be able to see through a vampire's illusion. If luck was on their side, the people who were after Trisha wouldn't have that particular skill.

Being sensitive to magic didn't equate with being able to see through illusions. And there were many different flavors of magic. Vampires worked on a whole different level than most human mages or most shifters, for that matter. They had a charm all their own.

"Activity," Mag reported quietly over his tac radio. "Billings. South-east corner."

Steve moved so he could see through the crowd. He was quite a distance away—they all were—but keen shifter eyesight allowed him to see clearly. Sure enough, there was the man of the hour, moving in on Trisha from across the street.

"Stay by the rail of the lake," her father instructed. "He coming in from the east. Jim and Rick are in the lake. They're your ace in the hole."

"Dammit, Dad. You spring this on me now? I can handle this on my own, you know."

"Who are Jim and Rick?" Steve asked, too distracted by the fact that the admiral had apparently brought his own team—and opted not to come clean about them until now—to keep the channel clear.

"My brothers," Trisha replied in a huffy tone. "It's a regular family reunion, apparently."

Then Steve remembered the seldom-mentioned Morrow brothers. Deke had talked about them only once that Steve could recall. They were Navy SEALs and the family wasn't encouraged to discuss them. In fact, the one time Deke had mentioned them after a few too many beers, he'd come back the next day and asked Steve to keep that info under his hat. Steve had understood. Spec Ops had to be low key. He'd lived in the community a long time. He knew there were different levels of secrecy, and he surmised that whatever Deke's brothers were into, it had to be way above Steve's pay grade.

Steve sent a communication directly to the admiral. "These are *your* sons, right? Same as you?"

"Affirmative," came the terse reply.

It made Steve feel a lot better to know that two highly trained and highly magical men were out there in the water—which was their element, after all—ready to help Trisha if she needed it. It also irked him that the old man hadn't seen fit to disclose this information up front, and he knew Trisha was going to be royally pissed at her dad. So the news was both welcome and irritating.

Trisha leaned over the rail of the big manmade lake. There was a fountain show here every hour, but they were in an off-time now, which meant the usual crowd hadn't gathered. Steve was glad. She reached over the rail as if to trail her fingers in the water and he could hear her soft words, directed at the SEALs who were completely hidden in the shallow lake.

"I'm real happy you guys are here, but let me handle this, okay? It's my battle, though I wouldn't mind a little discrete backup."

Steve didn't know if they answered somehow, but he got the feeling Trisha knew they could hear her. Maybe these beings who had such an affinity for water could use it somehow to help them communicate. He'd already heard the admiral's claim that the water could provide information to him. The idea was both fascinating and a little disconcerting. Steve had never thought of water as being alive—or at least sentient in some way.

Steve approached from the west and the bad guy was

coming in from the east. From across the street, at least a half dozen men were walking with purpose in their steps, directly toward Trisha.

"Incoming from the north," Steve informed the group over the tac radio. The lake was to the south and Trisha was back up against it. Steve looked behind him and noticed a few people walking his direction. One of them had his hands in the air and his gaze was focused on Trisha. "Slade, what's this guy behind me doing with his hands?"

"Nothing good. Take him down fast and clean, if you can. I'm coming." Slade was across the street, at least two hundred yards away. But Slade could *see* magic.

Steve knew a lot of human mages had to wave their hands in the air to conjure. Or maybe it was just an affectation. Whatever it was, this guy was doing it and Slade had confirmed it was magic. He had to be taken out. Steve stopped moving and pretended to bend down to tie his shoe. The mage stepped around him and kept going, which was his mistake.

Steve jumped him from behind, but the man didn't go down as easily as Steve expected. No, the guy turned the magic he'd been calling on Steve, and in the blink of an eye, the tables had turned.

Not in Steve's favor.

Trisha felt something happen. She didn't have the same kind of eyesight that shifters seemed to have, but she could use the water to see. The manmade lake here extended the length of the block. She reached out to it and saw Steve on the ground, held there by something that the water found evil. Impure.

Magic.

"Steve?" She wanted to run to him.

"Don't you dare." Her father's stern voice in her ear stopped her from following the impulse. "He's getting help better able to deal with this than you, little lady."

She hated it when he called her that.

But even as she watched through the water, she could feel the purity of the magic that approached. She looked up to see Slade at the farthest reaches of her vision. She squinted as the mysterious shifter moved fast in Steve's direction. The water liked him. It even—respected?—his magic. Steve would have good help. Her dad was right.

But that didn't stop her worry. Or her being distracted.

"You're a hard woman to track down." A new voice sounded from her side, approaching fast. She turned to see a stranger approaching as if he knew her. And she realized he did. This was the man they were all trying to stop. The magic sensor—Jeffrey Billings. And he'd taken her by surprise.

She'd been so worried about Steve, the rest of the night's mission had left her mind almost completely. Her brothers would kick her ass if they knew. And dammit, they were all watching. They probably knew. She'd never live this down. If she survived.

She had to salvage this somehow. Go on the offensive.

"So, Mr. Billings, we finally meet face-to-face." She felt satisfaction as his step faltered just the tiniest bit at the sound of his name. "That's far enough." She held one hand out, using the slight mist in the air generated by the fountains behind her to form a slight barrier. He seemed surprised enough to stop about four feet away from her.

"You do have skills. I thought you were just a passive." He frowned and his expression didn't look quite sane to her for a moment there. Then he seemed to refocus on her. "No matter. I have enough backup this time to get you and take all your power for my own."

Now *that* didn't sound good. She had to stall for time and try to draw more information out of him. They needed to know why he was doing this and who his friends were. Until they knew that, the threat would still exist even if they took him out.

"Won't your backup, as you call him, want you to share? I'm sure he's demanding something from you for his help."

"That's none of your business, tramp. I'll have you and

your power. What I do with it is my business."

"I'm afraid you're wrong." She was proud of how cool her voice sounded when she was trembling inside. It was all she could do to keep her knees from shaking visibly. She'd never had to confront anyone quite like this in her life. It was terrifying and kind of exhilarating all at the same time. "I won't go quietly, and if you attempt to take me, I'll have to object. Rather strongly, actually."

She pretended to buff her fingernails against her opposite sleeve. In reality, it was a signal they'd worked out in advance to begin tightening the noose around their target. Every shifter on the street had been watching and waiting for that signal and they all began a slow prowl closer while the vampires held the illusion of normalcy for the sake of the human populace.

"Your parlor tricks aren't going to stop me. In addition to being sensitive to magic, I'm also pretty much impervious to it." He walked right through her barrier and took hold of her wrist in a bruising grip. He smiled at her and her blood ran cold. That was an evil smile if she ever saw one. "One of my little gifts." He quirked his head to the side and seemed to chuckle.

Just her luck, this nutball was riding the crazy train. The look in his eyes and his actions to date told her he wasn't quite what you would call stable.

"So you just work for the *Venifucus*, then? You're a pawn but not an actual man of power. Pity." She used her most insulting tone and was gratified when his spine stiffened in offense. His brutal grip on her wrist tightened too, but she did her best not to grimace at the pain.

"I don't work for *them*." His outraged whisper was even more effective than if he had shouted. "They work for me."

"You're a fool if you believe that." She held his gaze, looking for any sign of weakness—or sanity.

"Don't call me a fool. You're the one who will die by my hand. After I've drained you of all your power."

"To what end? What are you going to do with all that

magic? If you're not a mage, what are you?"

"I never said I wasn't a mage. I am descended from one of the oldest bloodlines in Europe. I just don't have a lot of my own power. But I've learned how to drain it from Others. Like I will drain yours and claim it for my own."

Oh yeah, he was definitely loony tunes.

"You've done this before," she concluded.

Trying to turn someone else's magic to your own purposes against the will of the original being was not for the faint of heart—or the weak of mind. That was something Slade had mentioned when they'd been talking about magic earlier. She still had a lot to learn about this new world, but Trisha thought she knew what had happened to the pathetic creature who had hold of her arm. He'd driven himself crazy trying to tame other people's magic. Magic he was never meant to wield.

"Many times," he confirmed. "You don't stand a chance. It's cute of you to try and stop me, but you won't win in the end."

"We'll just have to see about that." She could see the deadness in his eyes now. The utter loss of whatever spark of humanity had once lived there. What he'd done to others had snapped back on him until he'd lost his mind.

"You're coming with me, one way or another. Let's go."

Trisha planted her feet even as he yanked on her arm. She used the strength of the water behind her to help her hold her position. The fine mist in the air made it almost impossible for him to pull her anywhere.

"I'm not going anywhere with you." She sent him a smile that seemed to infuriate him. He yanked harder and the mist—of which there was precious little in this desert climate—started to give way.

*Dammit.* Trisha redoubled her efforts to hold herself close to the water. If he managed to pull her away from it, she'd be lost. She needed the water. It was her power. Her life. Her magic.

He stopped pulling but didn't let her go. He was very

angry and his face was red with emotion and the effort he'd expended trying to pull her.

"Fine. We'll do this the messy way then."

He turned his head slightly and let loose and ear-splitting whistle. Trisha winced at the sound even as she noticed a number of large men emerging from the crowd around her. They were focused on Billings, which was probably why they weren't affected by the illusion the vampires continued to maintain. Other people walking on the Strip didn't seem to see the confrontation, but the men who'd been so focused on her would-be attacker weren't susceptible to the subtle mental suggestion of the vampires. Or, at least, the half-dozen men who were heading straight for her didn't seem to be affected.

They came toward her—three on the right and three on the left. Her heart sank and she knew she couldn't handle this alone. She sent a simple pulse of thought through the water, knowing her brothers would understand. They were ready to act—she could feel their watching presence hidden beneath the calm waters of the manmade lake. They were only holding off for the right moment.

As Billings tugged at her again and his henchmen drew near, all hell suddenly broke loose. Water erupted out of the lake behind her, a wave on her right and one on her left. And riding those waves were her brothers, Jimmy and Rick. They used the water to propel them up and over the railing as if they were surfing, only there were no boards involved.

When they hit the pavement, their clothing was dry and the water went neatly back into the lake...mostly. Some of it wrapped around their opponents. Or at least, it tried to. A trick she'd seen her brothers practice a million times didn't seem to want to work. Somehow, the henchmen were warded against magic.

But that wasn't a problem. Her brothers didn't have to rely on magic alone. They were well able to take on three goons each hand-to-hand. It would just take a little longer to mop the floor with them. That was all.

Or so she hoped.

# CHAPTER NINE

Slade arrived just as Steve started to feel the effects of some kind of paralyzing spell the mage had been trying to cast at Trisha. In one way, he was glad to take the brunt of it, but the dying need to get to his mate clawed at his insides. Steve didn't have all that much protection against this kind of magic. It had a lesser effect on him than it probably would have had on a human, but he was still having real trouble with it.

He saw the mage smile as he went down on one knee before him. Steve didn't like it. His Alpha nature bowed to no man—especially not this evil thing that had tried to hurt Trisha. He fought against the magic, moving steadily closer and allowing his hands to shift into the battle form claws that could do so much damage.

Given a single chance, Steve would gladly sink his claws deep into the evil man's flesh, rending and tearing, showing no mercy. He only needed a single break in the debilitating magic that held him back.

"Hold him there, buddy. I'm coming up from behind." Slade's voice sounded in Steve's ear over the tac radio. Steve felt a moment's triumph. A little assist was all he needed. "I'll go high," Slade said, and it was music to Steve's ears. He poised to strike.

As one of Slade's arms snaked around the mage's neck and the other yanked one arm back hard, breaking the spell, Steve struck at his legs, claws sinking deep. The mage's scream satisfied the cat as he pounced with Slade, taking the mage to the ground in a bloody heap.

"I've got him," Slade said quickly. "The spell is broken and he won't be casting any others. Go help your mate."

Gratified by the backup, though the cat wanted to kill, Steve turned and ran for Trisha. In the short moments he'd been incapacitated, the situation had gotten considerably worse.

She was fighting Billing's hold on her arm, not giving too much ground, Steve was glad to see, but those six henchmen were closing in fast. And then there was a wave—an actual wave of water—that rose from the lake behind her. It deposited two burly men in fatigues, one on each side of Trisha, and Steve knew they had to be her brothers.

Sure enough, even as he ran toward them, the two warriors engaged with the goons. They waded in with fists and feet, taking three attackers each and doing very well, but they wouldn't be fast enough. Billings still had hold of Trisha and was making some headway in hauling her along with him.

He'd already pulled her several yards down the block, away from the ongoing battle and they seemed to be picking up momentum. Steve put on a burst of speed and adjusted his angle of attack.

Leaping through the air using all of his skill and agility, he dove for Billings, coming in from the side. He knocked the man off his feet and the great momentum carried them both over the railing and right into the lake. The water churned around them as they fell in, disorienting Steve for a moment while he tried to figure out which end was up and where his prey had gone.

Steve liked the water, but he'd never really had to fight in it before. It would take a moment to adjust. He just hoped he had a moment to spare.

Trisha gasped as Billing's hand wrenched her arm and then lost its grip. She watched in shock as Steve appeared, flying through the air from out of nowhere to tackle Billings and take him right over the rail. She ran to the rail and watched them both fall in a writhing tangle into the lake.

Trisha didn't think twice. She hopped up on the rail and dove in after them. She could handle just about anything in the water, but she worried for Steve. She'd only just found him. She couldn't bear the thought of losing him so soon. She loved him.

That thought clear in her mind, Trisha waited for the bubbles to clear and nearly gasped at what she saw. Billings had somehow reversed positions and was doing his best—which was surprisingly good—to drown Steve.

Fury took over. Fury fueled by fear for the man she loved with all her heart. Trisha called on the water as she had never done before, asking it to separate the men and sweep the evil one away, holding him far from her and Steve. Currents began to build and only a moment later—though it felt like an eternity—the water complied.

Steve was freed from Billings's hold and he pushed for the surface, in desperate need of air. Trisha swam over to him, staying beneath the surface for now, keeping an eye on Billings. She didn't want him to get away.

There were two splashes and her brothers appeared at her side. She pointed to where Billings thrashed against the current she had created and Jim smiled. Rick started swimming toward Billings while Jim motioned for her to rise to the surface. His gestures told her they would take care of Billings.

Glad to be rid of the duty and certain her brothers would know what to do with the man, Trisha followed her heart to the surface…and Steve. She swam upward, right into his waiting arms, and she'd never felt anything better than his embrace.

"Are we clear? I saw your brothers go in," he asked, even as he held her tight.

"They're taking care of Billings. I held him in a current, but Jim and Rick are better at that kind of thing than I am. They do it for a living. I'm just an amateur."

"You're amazing, Trisha." His words touched her deeply.

"I love you, Steve."

She kissed him with so much emotion little swirls of energy filled the water around them, cocooning them in a safe, protected circle where nothing could come between them. They were alone in the universe—and the entire Las Vegas Strip.

When Steve released her finally, after long, pleasurable, emotion-filled moments, Trisha suddenly realized that while the vampires were shielding them from human view, there was a whole contingent of Others—shapeshifters, vampires and their allies—who could, and did, see them. Many curious stares were focused on her.

She ducked a little behind Steve, but it didn't help all that much. There were still a lot of interested eyes on them.

"Um... I think we should probably get out of here." She could feel the heat of a blush in her cheeks.

"Can you do that wave thing like your brothers?" he asked, almost daring her.

"Yes, but...it's a little showy. And everybody's watching." Her gaze darted toward the onlookers, then she looked downward, self-conscious. But Steve placed one finger under her chin and coaxed her to raise her gaze to meet his.

"All the more reason to show off a little. Shifter society is all about hierarchy. Since you can't shift, you need to earn the Clan's respect in another way. You've gone a long way toward doing that here tonight, so why not finish strong?" His gaze dared her to give it a try and she'd always loved a dare.

"Okay. Just hang on, and I'll have us on the sidewalk in a jiff." She held his hand tight.

With her free hand, she made a tiny wave in the water at her side and put some of her power behind it until it grew to a towering height that lifted them up and over the railing. It deposited them on their feet on the sidewalk and then she sent the water back into the lake, thanking it for its assistance with a thought.

If every other magical creature on the Strip hadn't been watching before, they certainly were now. Keeping Steve's words about hierarchy in mind, she kept her chin up and her head held high. She looked over at him and saw the wide grin on his face even as he scanned the crowd, making sure they were safe.

He was such a good man. Such a fierce protector. A great lover. And the best friend she thought she'd ever have. Even after such a short time together, she knew in her heart they were on the same wavelength. They'd shared a lot in a compressed time, but even more than that, she knew him for the match to her soul she'd hoped—but never quite dared believe—she'd find.

Steve was it for her. Her man. Her mate.

After tonight, any tiny remaining doubt had been laid to rest.

With a quick burst of her magic, she dried them both, sending the moisture back into the lake. Just that short contact with the lake water told her something she had expected but had hoped wouldn't happen. She shuddered.

"What?" Steve asked, sensitive to her moods. He'd probably felt her shiver through their joined hands.

"Billings is dead. He refused to be subdued, and in the struggle the water claimed him."

The look in Steve's eyes held both compassion and a determined sort of satisfaction. "I'm not sorry the threat he posed to you is at an end, but it would have been good to be able to question him." Steve would have said more, but his brother Mag walked over, accompanied by a distinguished-looking man and a gorgeous, fragile female.

"I'm Miranda." The woman reached out first, introducing herself to Trisha. "Your power is impressive."

"Indeed," the older man added, nodding in a very old-world way. "I suggest we move off the street. My people have strong influence over humans, but we cannot be sure there are not Others watching our every move."

He made a gesture and Trisha started walking, surrounded by the small group. They headed for the hotel they'd been in earlier and nobody spoke until they were inside. Trisha kept looking over at Miranda and Mag. They seemed cozy and Mag's attention to the other woman's frailty was almost touching to see. Yet she sensed some reserve surrounded the couple. Some kind of unspoken or unresolved feelings that kept them on edge around each other.

Trisha was also fascinated by the idea that the woman and the older man were vampires. She'd never thought such creatures were real. Her father had done a good job of closing her off from even the possibility of magic other than her own. She felt kind of stupid now, of course. But all her life, her father had been her guide, her teacher, her rock. Now though, she saw him as a man. A powerful man, of course, but still a man who occasionally made bad decisions.

Keeping her in the dark for so long was probably his worst idea ever, and it would take time before she was willing to forgive him for that one. Of course, she had Steve now. And although she knew she could lean on his strength, he also gave her freedom to be who she was and use her abilities. He'd given her wings.

And she would always love him for that. That and so much more.

When they arrived at the suite of rooms they had used before, near the top of the high-rise hotel, there was already a crowd gathered and more arrived with every elevator. Magnus and his friend Miranda talked quietly with Trisha and Steve, introducing the older man as the Master vampire of the area. He was formal at first but then invited her to call him Tony, which judging by the raised eyebrows all around was something of a surprise.

She was standing, talking with Tony about what his people had done to obscure the action on the street when her family arrived. Her father walked right up to her and swept her into a giant hug, which was rare for him. He usually wasn't one to show emotion or affection easily. The slight tremble in his strong arms spoke volumes to her about how worried he'd been.

"You did good, munchkin," he whispered to her before letting her go.

She went from her dad to her brothers, as one by one they all gave her hugs and pats on the back. They looked at her with new respect—something that hadn't been there before. Maybe she'd finally been able to prove her mettle to them. Just as she'd proved it to herself.

When they finally let her go, she made the introductions as her newly arrived brothers said hello to those who had been in on the operation from the beginning. Grif frowned when he shook hands with Jim and Rick. Trisha understood his concern. Her father had been highhanded as usual, keeping secrets and men in reserve from the rest of the operation. His methods weren't always aboveboard, but they always got results.

"Shall we do the debriefing here?" her father asked in his command voice, leaving little choice. But all eyes turned to Grif. He was the Alpha in charge here—not her dad—for a change.

"Might as well. We probably won't all be gathered together like this for a while." Grif led the way to the large table that filled one corner of the giant suite.

The inlaid wooden table could be used for dining or as a conference table. It would just fit all the players in tonight's action, with some people perched on the credenza behind it and others dragging chairs from other parts of the suite over, to be within earshot. Looking around, she realized there had to be at least thirty people in the room and a few more coming in from the balcony. She frowned, trying to understand what so many people had been doing on the balcony all this time.

Steve must've seen her confusion. He dipped his head near her ear and whispered. "Raptors. They were acting as air support."

Bird shifters. Well, that was pretty cool. And yet another facet of this magical world she hadn't known existed.

When everyone had settled, Grif, sitting at the head of the table, began to speak. "I'd like to personally thank everyone who assisted here tonight. Master Antoinne, please pass my thanks and the gratitude of the Redstone Clan on to your people. We could not have done this without their assistance." Grif indicated the Master vampire with a respectful nod of his head. "Perhaps you could start the debrief by telling us how much damage control we may need to do in the coming days?"

"Certainly," Tony replied, his cultured and rich voice spilling out into the room. The man oozed elegance but with a deadly edge. "The elders of my forces were engaged in active illusion while the younger and less adept with such things were set to watch. We had only three instances where otherwise normal humans noticed some of the action. Each was intercepted and evaluated. Two were bespelled into forgetfulness. The other is still with one of my operatives. It is a woman. Her mind is resistant." Tony gave a slight frown. "I will go have a look at her as soon as we're done here and see what I might be able to do to mitigate the problem. Maybe one of your people would like to accompany me? The snowcat or his mate, perhaps?"

Both Slade and Kate nodded from the other side of the table. "We'd be glad to assist. The more we can hide what happened here tonight, the better for all of us."

Tony nodded. "Other than the three humans, only agents of the enemy saw what happened. All of those are accounted for—either dead or awaiting our questioning. They have been taken to a remote location and will remain under guard there until we are ready to talk to them."

"I'll need to take a look at them too," Kate put in. "To see if any of them bear the *Venifucus* tattoos. Slade and I can see them where most beings can't."

"Your assistance in this matter would be most helpful, Priestess. Thank you." Tony sat down with only a slight flourish and everyone's attention turned back to Grif.

"Containment was my immediate concern. It sounds like your people have a good handle on that, Tony. Next, I'd like to discuss parameters. Admiral Morrow." Grif turned to Trisha's father with a very stern expression. "While I appreciate your reputation for strategy and experience, I will not allow you to operate within my realm of influence again unless I have your assurance that all your assets will be disclosed up front. Keeping your sons in reserve is something I can understand, but it caused confusion for my people and nearly caused your sons to come under attack before we realized what was going on."

"I'd have liked to see them try," Jim whispered. He'd always been a wiseass and every shifter in the room had to have heard his snide comment. It was obvious they had—they all bristled.

"We were above you, moron," a man seated on the credenza behind them said. "Ever seen an eagle dive on salmon?"

Jim turned in his seat, giving the guy who'd spoken a hard look. "Redstones are cougars."

Every shifter in the room made a scoffing sound.

"My family is cougar, that's true," Grif said slowly, as if speaking to a child—a stupid child, at that. "But Redstone Construction—which essentially *is* the Clan—encompasses shifters of all kinds. Raptors especially like to walk the iron. You escaped being clawed by the skin of your teeth."

Understanding dawned on Jim's face. Rick also looked a little taken aback, though he was always harder to read.

"My apologies, Alpha," her father finally replied. He'd given every shifter in the room a quick, evaluating glance. If she was any judge of her father's expressions, he was impressed. "I didn't have time to brief them fully."

Trisha was surprised. It wasn't often that her father admitted he might have made a mistake.

"Now that's out of the way." Grif took back control of the debrief. "What did you do with Billings?"

"He refused to stop struggling and drowned," Rick reported.

"His body is in the back of a van Slade pointed us toward before we came up," Jim added. Everyone's attention turned to Slade.

"One of Tony's people took him out to where they're keeping the prisoners. We need to examine him for tattoos before we dispose of the body," Slade put in.

Grif nodded, seemingly satisfied with the results. "We need to know how deeply involved he was with the *Venifucus*, if at all possible. I don't like how active they've been in our area in the past few months. We've struck a blow against them here tonight, but there have to be more of them out there plotting against us. I want to know all we can about them before we have to face them again."

There were nods all around as the shifters and vamps agreed with the Alpha's words.

"All right. Anything else we need to discuss before we all go our separate ways?" Grif asked. Nobody came forward, and the overall feeling in the room was one of relief, satisfaction and fatigue. It was late and people wanted to go about their normal lives. Trisha could get behind that idea. Big time.

"Then thanks again and let's disperse a few at a time. You know the drill." Grif rose and went to talk with Kate and Slade for a moment as some of his people stopped briefly to say goodbye as they headed out.

Trisha watched a few of the men she thought had to be bird shifters head toward the balcony. Through the tinted window, she could just make out the movements as they discarded their clothing, folded it and put it in a big satchel. One of the others took the satchel and came back into the room. He was still carrying it as he left the suite. Apparently he was going to take the birdmen's clothes back home while they shifted and flew.

She couldn't really see them shapeshift in the dark and through tinted glass, but she was able to make out large feathered wings as they launched, one by one, from the balcony railing. Steve squeezed her hand as he rose and she stood up automatically, following his lead. She was still fascinated by the idea of people being able to turn into birds and fly away, but her father was standing in front of her and she knew she had to focus.

"When are you coming home, Trisha?" her father asked.

Taken aback, Trisha didn't know what to say. "We still have another few days here in Vegas," she temporized. "And Steve and I need to discuss a few things."

She felt his hand tighten on hers and she knew she'd said the right thing. He was remaining suspiciously silent, letting her handle her family, and she was grateful for it. She needed to assert herself with the men in her family. If she didn't do it now, she never would. And that was no way to start a new life.

She'd changed on a fundamental level tonight. She'd finally stood on her own. She'd faced her fears. She'd faced danger. And she'd learned things about herself and her abilities. Things that would never be forgotten now they were out in the open. She couldn't go back to being the biddable little sister or daughter who let the big, strong men of her family take care of everything.

"I see." Her father frowned a little, but for once, she didn't let his apparent disapproval affect her decisions.

She was her own woman now. She had proved it to herself—and to anyone who had been watching. If her dad needed time to figure that out, she'd give it to him. He was her dad, after all, but he would no longer control every aspect of her life. Those days were over.

"I'm glad you do." She stepped forward and hugged him. "I love you, Daddy. I always will. But I'm not a little girl anymore. I've grown up."

She stepped back and her brother Rick stepped in to defuse the moment. "You can say that again. Trish, you did great tonight. I didn't even realize you knew half those tricks. You're a force to be reckoned with, sis." He gave her a quick hug that made her laugh and stepped back. And just like that, the tense moment had passed.

"Are you going to stay for a while?" she asked.

She didn't see a lot of her brothers nowadays. They were always off saving one part of the world or another. She worried for them, but she knew they had skills she couldn't even imagine. As long as they were in or near water, they would be okay.

"I think we'll probably be in Las Vegas until your friends are on the plane home." Rick winked at her and she was very aware of the way he'd phrased his words.

If things worked out as she hoped they would, she wouldn't be on the plane with her friends. She'd be staying right here with Steve. But they hadn't talked logistics yet, and she knew they had some things to work out before she knew where she'd be headed in the next few days.

"I just got a call from the Pack house. Your friends are waking up. Everybody seems fine, if a little confused. I'm heading over there now." Kate stopped for a moment to talk before heading out of the suite with Slade.

Trisha looked over at Steve and he nodded. She didn't even need to say the words. She knew that he knew what was on her mind.

"We'll come too. What are we going to tell them?"

"Maybe some kind of bug? What do you think, Doc?" Slade asked Trisha as he slung one arm around his mate's shoulders.

"That could work. Maybe." Trisha frowned, thinking about what she could plausibly tell her human friends about why they'd been unconscious for so long.

"We could reinforce whatever story you come up with using a touch of magic. Your fey friend might even be of some help there," Kate mused. "I'll call ahead and tell Lynda to meet us in the front room before we go up so we can coordinate."

Trisha nodded. She hated lying to her friends, but she also needed to protect everyone—the shifters, the vampires, everyone in the Redstone Clan and her human friends too. The less her friends knew about what had really happened here in Vegas, the better for everyone. This time, that saying about *what happened in Vegas* was definitely true.

Kate and Slade left a moment later and Kate was on her phone even as they walked out the door. Trisha was glad she was organizing things. She'd been a huge help with everything and Trisha felt genuine affection for the other woman. She thought they could be good friends, given half a chance.

She watched them go and then turned back to Steve as he squeezed her elbow.

"Jim and Rick are going directly before us, and your father and Deke will act as rearguard. Of course, Grif is guarding the rear of the rearguard." Steve chuckled. "But the admiral doesn't need to know that. We have more than enough firepower out and about tonight to handle just about anything that might pop up. And I truly believe the main threat has been neutralized."

"But there could be more enemies out there?" She hadn't really thought about that too much. She'd been trying not to.

"When you're a shifter—or have magic of any kind—and serve the Light, there are always enemies." Steve sighed. "It's the age-old battle between good and evil. We live it every day of our lives. We're much closer to it than most beings in this realm, and we are held to a higher standard than most because of our abilities and beliefs. Kate will tell you all about it…if you stay."

And there it was. The question of the hour. Of the day. Of her life.

"Do you want me to stay?" she whispered, not caring where they were or who might be watching them. This was too important.

Steve took both of her hands in his own gentle grip. "I want you with me for the rest of my days, Trisha. You're my mate. My love. The only one for me. Without you, I am incomplete. Of course I want you to stay. I want you to stay for the rest of our lives."

The moment was precious to her. Precious and magical. As if the entire universe boiled down to just the two of them, together, in this special moment.

"I can do that. I love you too, Steve." She reached up on tiptoe, smiling all the while, and kissed him on the lips, giggling when he snaked his arms around her waist and lifted her clear off her feet as the kiss deepened.

Dimly, in the background, she heard a few hoots and hollers and one long, piercing wolf whistle that eventually drew them apart. Steve was smiling down at her and she couldn't contain the joy she felt inside. She laughed as those left in the room began congratulating them, clapping Steve on the back and wishing them well. He let her go, but not far, keeping his arm around her shoulders as people stopped and welcomed her to the Clan.

Jim and Rick had already left, but her dad and Deke were there when the initial cheering died down. Deke punched Steve in the arm a little harder than was probably necessary, but Steve didn't budge. The smile on Deke's face was a little pained, but it was definitely a smile. He would come around, Trisha knew. Eventually.

"When I asked you to look after my little sister, I didn't mean for you to propose, dirt bag. Now I suppose I'll have to stomach you as a brother-in-law—or whatever it is you shifters call it."

"Same as humans," Steve said. "She'll be my wife and you'll be my brother-in-law. You'll even have a place in the Clan, if you want it, I suppose. We're going to have to talk to Grif about that. We have a couple of non-magic folk in the Clan already, but they're special cases. I guess you'll be too, if you want it."

"Are you kidding?" This time Deke's smile even wider. "I've been surrounded by magic folk most of my life, on the outside looking in. I wouldn't pass up a chance to rub elbows with some of your shifter ladies. From the few I've seen, they are *fine*." Trisha laughed at his exaggerated antics and so did Steve, thank goodness.

"That's all I need. More shifters in the family," her father griped, pushing Deke aside as he faced them. His glower wasn't nearly as bad as she'd feared it would be. Still, she just knew he was going to give Steve a hard time. "I'll expect you at our family home next week. All the boys are on leave—barring any major difficulties in the world—and I want a chance for my wife to meet you before the wedding. And you *will* have a wedding. I've done my best to give Trisha and the boys a normal life despite our gifts. I expect you to do the same, young man."

"Yes, sir. If Trisha wants a human-style wedding, that's what we'll have. White dress, thousands of flowers that'll make me sneeze and everything." Steve looked down at her and winked.

"Well, maybe not *thousands* of flowers," Trisha spoke softly, smiling up at him. "Maybe just a few. And we'll try for varieties that won't make you sneeze. But I know Mom would love to plan a wedding, and I've dreamed of it since I was a little girl. So yeah, I want one. Just something small with our families in attendance and a big party after the ceremony."

"Whatever you want, sweetheart," Steve promised, and she knew he meant more than just the proposed wedding. He would give her anything her heart desired. Luckily, all she really wanted or needed in the whole world was him.

# CHAPTER TEN

Steve felt like he was walking on air as he escorted Trisha into the Pack house a short while later. She'd agreed to be his mate. Sure, he'd have to give her a human ceremony, but he was almost looking forward to it. Anything that made her happy made him happy too. If she wanted a special day and a frilly white dress, he'd make it happen. He'd do anything for her. Absolutely anything.

Behind them, her family and his were mingling, talking over security details. He knew Grif was going to make sure the Morrows were introduced to the wolf Alphas and some of the wolf Pack. Grif would keep the Morrow men entertained while Trisha dealt with her friends.

The first stop was a quick *tete a tete* with Lynda in the front parlor. She was waiting for them when they arrived, nervously wringing her hands and pacing. She was a little thing, Steve mused, with a kind of ethereal beauty that should have tipped him off as to her Other status. But then again, since he'd first seen Trisha, he'd had eyes only for her. So the fey woman had slipped right under his radar.

The women hugged as they met in the middle of the room. It was a brief greeting filled with relief on the fey's part, if he was any judge. They sat down and he joined them, taking his place at Trisha's side. He saw the way Lynda's gaze

140

went from Trisha to him and back again, one eyebrow raised in question, but he only smiled.

"What have you told the girls so far?" Trisha asked, bringing the reason for their hasty meeting into focus.

"Not much. They were still very groggy when I got word you were coming. I left them in one of the sitting rooms and came to meet you. I just said they'd been sick and that you'd explain it all when you got here. I didn't know what else to do."

Trisha took a deep breath and Steve could tell from the look on her face and the set of her shoulders that she wasn't thrilled to have the entire burden thrust upon her, but she'd deal with it. His mate was a trooper.

"All right. We'll say they all caught the same bug and that they had such high fevers that they weren't quite coherent. That's why they can't remember anything. What do you think?"

"I think it could work," Lynda said slowly, though she looked skeptical.

"Can you reinforce the story with your magic?" Steve asked point blank. The fey woman might try to pass as human, but she wasn't. And neither was Trisha. There was no sense pretending otherwise.

She looked at him sharply, her eyes narrowing. It took her a moment to reply, but when she did, she had seemed to come to some kind of decision.

"I don't generally go about manipulating people I consider friends, but I can see that this is a special circumstance. The less they know about what happened to them—or about the den of shifters they've landed in—the better. Right?"

"That about sums it up," Steve agreed. "And for the sake of your friendship with these ladies…" Steve included Trisha in his observation, "…it's probably best they never realize the magic you both bear."

"Good call," Trisha approved, placing one hand on his knee and squeezing gently.

It was such a casual touch, but it set him aflame with

wanting. It also filled him with a sense of happiness, of possession and of pride. That this special woman touched him so casually meant more than he could say. She'd staked her claim on him in front of her friend and she probably hadn't even realized she was doing it. That meant something to him. It meant a *lot*, actually.

This having-a-mate stuff was going to take some getting used to, but he looked forward eagerly to every moment, every lesson in being part of a duo. Forever. His life joined to hers, never to part in this realm or the next.

Trisha might not have a full grasp of what mating meant to shifters, but over the years she would figure it out. It would be his pleasure to teach her the ways of his people and he looked forward to learning more about her magic and her abilities. Fate had handed him one hell of a woman.

The women talked over the details of their story for a few minutes more, but it was easy to see that both were eager to check on their friends. Steve followed them up the stairs to the wing of rooms the humans had been given to use. There was a lot more activity in the area as the ladies walked freely between rooms.

They had all gathered in the sitting area of the rooms that had been given to the bride-to-be, Marcia Parkhurst. Steve knew her father was an oilman in Texas and it was his money that had financed this junket.

When the women saw their two friends walk in, their voices rose in welcome. Hugs were passed out as Steve watched discretely from the partially open door. He observed without being seen as Trisha explained the illness they had suffered, even giving it a technical name and explaining in medical terms what it had done to them and why they didn't remember much.

When Marcia asked where they were, Steve heard his cue to join the conversation. He knocked on the door, swinging it open a little as he alerted them to his presence.

"Is it okay if I come in?" he asked politely. He didn't miss the speculative glances aimed at him from most of the women in the room, but he only had eyes for Trisha.

"Everybody, this is Red. He's a former colleague of my brother, Deke's. He was kind enough to come to our rescue when I realized I needed help. Luckily, he lives here in Las Vegas and his family was in a position to be able to help us. Deke had given me his number in case of emergencies and boy, was I glad I had someone local to call on."

Marcia rose and extended a hand to Steve. She wasn't quite stable on her feet, so he went over to her to spare her having to walk any distance. He shook her hand and smiled, acting the part Trisha had devised for him. Rescuer. Friend of the family. He could play that part easily.

"It's a pleasure to see you all up and around, finally. I was very worried there for a while, but Trisha assured me she had your health problems under control." He turned on the charm to win over Trisha's friends. From the looks on their faces, that wasn't too hard to do.

"So where are we?" Marcia repeated. "This isn't the hotel."

"It's a boarding house of sorts," Steve explained. "It belongs to my family's company." He didn't say *Clan*, though the company and Clan were pretty much one and the same these days. "Trisha sometimes calls me Red because that was my nickname in the service and that's what Deke always calls me, but my proper name is Steve Redstone. I'm Chief Security Officer for my family's business, Redstone Construction."

The humans began to look impressed. There were few people in North America who hadn't heard of the company his parents had founded and that he and his brothers had turned into something much bigger than anyone had expected.

"My father had dealings with Redstone Construction. You built a housing development near one of his remote worksites so his workers could bring their families," Marcia drawled in her unmistakable Texan accent. "He was very pleased with the results, as I recall."

BIANCA D'ARC

"Glad to hear it," Steve answered politely as the woman sat back down. "As a rule, we like happy customers." He took the empty seat near Trisha as she made the introductions. After he had met everyone formally, talk turned to plans for the rest of their trip.

"I don't know how y'all feel," Marcia said, seeming to take charge of the room. "But I'm fine now and I feel cheated that we didn't get to see much of Las Vegas yet. If you're up for it, we can finish out our trip before heading back home. We still have show tickets and tours lined up. What do you say?"

They took a vote and everyone was in favor, but Steve didn't want to let them loose on the Strip again after everything that had happened. He had a plan.

"You have what...three more days in town?" Nods answered his question. "I'd like to propose a few minor changes. This is my hometown after all, and Redstone Construction has many assets at its disposal. I'd like to offer the company helicopter to give you an aerial tour." He could see the delight on the ladies' faces at mention of the private chopper. "And you may not remember them well, but you made some friends right before you were taken ill. The guys who helped bring you here were members of one of our crews who have worked for us for years. They're good men, and a few of them were very impressed with several of you ladies." Now he saw the flare of feminine interest on a few of their faces. "I'd like to offer them as escorts for the duration of your stay. They know the area and can take you anywhere you want to go. I'll even provide company cars."

"Why?" Marcia wondered aloud.

Steve appealed to the ladies' sense of romance by taking Trisha's hand. "Well, I admit to having a certain fondness for one of your group. I'd love a chance to spend more time with her." He looked deep into Trisha's eyes and brought her hand to his lips to kiss it tenderly. He could hear the sighs of the ladies watching and knew his little show was having the desired effect. But more than that, he meant every word he spoke. He would do anything to spend every moment for the rest of his life with her.

"Is that what you want, Trish?" Marcia asked bluntly, but Trisha was smiling at him as she nodded.

"More than anything." At her answer, his smile grew into a grin.

"Then I guess we accept your generous offer, Mr. Redstone. Thank you." Again, Marcia spoke for the group. He guessed as the bride-to-be this really was her show.

"Excellent." He let go of Trisha's hand slowly, savoring the feel of her skin against his. "I'll go make the arrangements while you all catch up. I'm sure you have lots to talk about. And please, call me Steve."

He stood and went to the door, pausing only to send Trisha a little wink that wasn't missed by the eagle-eyed ladies in the room. Good. He'd given them a distraction that might further enhance their belief in the yarn Trisha had spun about illness making them forget two days of their lives. His work here was done. For the moment.

It was well after midnight when the girls finally headed back to their rooms. It had been decided they would stay at the Pack house for the night and then decide whether to move back to their hotel on the Strip the next day. Trisha suspected that once the girls got a load of the shifter men— handsome as sin and built to drool over—they'd probably want to stay here. After all, besides Marcia they were all single.

Well, Trisha wasn't single anymore. No, now she had Steve, though her friends didn't quite realize how close they really were just yet. They'd figure it out sooner or later. When the time was right. She wanted to ease them into the idea that she'd found her life mate while they'd all been knocked out.

Trisha met Steve by the staircase. He looked like he'd been waiting for her and her heart lifted at the slight smile on his face when she appeared. It was a smile filled with love and acceptance of who she really was—something she'd dreamed about but never really thought she'd find. Steve knew everything about her now. He knew her deepest secret. He knew about her magic—and her family. And he loved her still.

Trisha had never thought she'd be able to be totally honest with a man, and yet, here he was. She'd been blessed with the hope of a future brighter than anything she'd ever expected. Now all they had to do was make it reality. Starting right now.

Trisha skipped the last few steps to him and launched herself into his arms. He caught her and clutched her close to his muscular body, warming her from within with his welcome. His mouth sought hers and she returned the welcome, kissing him deeply and raising her legs to circle his waist.

They were at the top of a staircase, in full view of anyone who might pass by, but she didn't care. It had been too long since she'd been in his arms. Too long since they'd made love. And after everything that had happened that night, her adrenaline was still running high. She wanted him. And she didn't want to wait.

Suddenly they were moving, but she didn't question whether or not he could support her. She knew he was strong. And he would never let her fall. He would take care of her. Always.

Including right now. A door opened and a moment later it closed behind them and her back was up against it. He broke the kiss and she glanced behind him. They were in one of the empty rooms on the same corridor where her friends were staying. She spared a single thought to hope that the walls were reasonably soundproof before throwing caution to the wind and pushing at Steve's shoulders. He was wearing way too many clothes.

He moved only a few inches away, but it was enough room for her to maneuver. She lowered her legs to the floor so she could stand and then went to work on his clothing. Her hands and arms tangled with his as each of them reached out to undress the other.

Somehow, finally, with a few laughs and some bumbles on

her part, she was naked and he was…naked enough. She didn't care if he still had his boots on and his pants were only partially lowered. The important part—the part she needed *right now*—was available and ready.

He pushed her against the door again and she went happily, hoisting her legs up and around his narrow hips. And then…bliss as he slid into her deep and true. He paused, both of them breathing hard, his forehead leaning against hers as they savored the moment.

"You are so perfect," he whispered, and she felt the truth of his words in her heart. *He* was the perfect one. Perfect for her. And together, they could move mountains.

She couldn't speak as he began moving, pushing deep and hitting a particular spot inside her in this position that nearly sent her into orbit with every thrust. She began to whimper and then moan, unable to hold in her cries of passion as she approached a very high peak in a very short time. She'd never been so hot, even with Steve—the most talented lover she'd ever had.

Maybe the danger they'd faced had given her some kind of edge. Maybe it was the novel position. Maybe it was the idea they were having a quickie in a place they really shouldn't— not with her friends such a short distance away. The naughtiness of it appealed to some previously unknown imp in her nature, she guessed. Whatever it was, she rode the wave into oblivion, crying out incoherently at the end as the most incredible sensations made her tingle all over.

She only barely registered that Steve came a moment after her. She was glad he'd joined her in that place that only he could take her. They were well matched in that regard and she knew it would make the rest of their relationship—the rest of their lives—easier to work out. They hadn't talked logistics yet, but she figured they'd each have to give a little ground to smooth things out and start a life together. But those heavy thoughts were for another time. A time when her mind hadn't just been blown to Mercury and back with a swing around the sun for good measure.

"That was incredible," she whispered when she was finally able to speak again. They were both still breathing hard but slowly coming back to earth.

"You rock my world, babe." Steve grinned, leaning in to kiss her sweetly even as he disengaged their bodies.

"Back at'cha, big guy." She smiled even as a suspicious wetness made her aware they hadn't used protection. Again. *Hmm.*

Well, she supposed they'd both been a little too eager to stop and think before they'd fucked like bunnies up against the door. And if she got pregnant, it wouldn't be the end of the world. In fact, it would be a new beginning for them. One of many they would have together, she was sure.

"Back in a minute." She scooted toward the attached bathroom, snagging the most important articles of her clothing along the way.

Only a tiny bit mortified but mostly thrilled and very, very satisfied, she spent a few minutes cleaning up. When she came back out, Steve was sitting on the bed looking at his smartphone. He had a serious expression on his face.

"Anything wrong?" she asked as she crossed the room.

He stood and his face lit with a gratifying pleasure as she walked up to him. He put his arms around her and hugged her, swaying a bit, making her feel cherished in a way she hadn't expected but knew she would come to crave given enough time with this man. A lifetime. That's what she wanted. A lifetime with him.

"Just checking on the interrogation. It's going as well as can be expected. I'll get a full report from Slade when they're done, but for now we still need to exercise caution. Slade doesn't think we got them all."

"Oh, no." Suddenly crashing back to the reality of the threat against her and her friends wasn't pleasant.

"Don't worry. You and your friends will be under guard twenty-four/seven. If anyone tries anything, I'll be right there to stop it. Me and about twenty of my best people. Around the clock. We've got you covered." He dropped a kiss on her forehead and set her away. "Okay?"

His words made her feel a lot better. Plus, she'd proven her own worth to herself, if not to everyone in her family and half of Steve's Clan, earlier that night. They could handle it.

"Now, we haven't been using protection. Are you okay with the possibility we could be starting a family before we even talked about it?" His eyes sought hers and held while he brought up the topic she'd been thinking about.

"Yeah, I'm okay with it. I've always wanted kids. I know it's a big step, but I'm committed to you and I know you are to me. It's the next logical step, though I didn't expect it so quickly. But if fate steps in, who am I to argue?"

Steve seemed to breathe a sigh of relief. "Thank goodness. I'm sorry, honey, I just wasn't thinking straight. I was so desperate to have you."

"I'm both flattered and in total agreement. I wasn't thinking either." She put one hand on his shoulder and stroked him lightly through the fabric of his shirt. "It's okay. We can be a little more careful, I guess, but if a baby comes of our love, I won't be upset."

"Good. Neither will I. In fact, I'd be pretty damn stoked." His eyes lit with momentary joy. "But I'm not in a hurry either. Kids will come when they come. As you say, it's up to the Mother of All ultimately. She's in charge."

Trisha realized another thing at that moment that she hadn't really considered—though she probably should have. "You follow the Goddess."

"Well, yeah. Kate's Her priestess. All were worship Her in one form or another, I think, as do most magic folk."

"That's great. I mean, Dad taught us about the Goddess and Mom was just hippie enough to go along. We don't advertise it, but we're definitely not in the mainstream religion-wise."

"You're mainstream for a shifter Clan." He chuckled and took her hand as they walked toward the door. "Don't worry. You'll fit right in."

He opened the door first, peeking out to see who might be

in the hall.

"The coast is clear," he whispered as he opened the door wider so they could slip out. She loved being able to laugh with him. Everything was so easy with Steve. Like they'd been best friends forever.

They weren't so lucky as they made their way down the stairs. Shifters had sharp senses and judging by the knowing grins of the few werewolves they passed on their way out, their little tryst hadn't gone unnoticed. Trisha was both embarrassed and amused.

"How do they know?" she whispered to him as he escorted her to his vehicle—a low-slung sports car she hadn't seen him drive before.

In answer, he simply tapped his nose. She cringed thinking how sensitive a werewolf's nose must be. If their human noses were anything like their wolf counterparts...well, they could tell what she and Steve had been up to. No doubt about it.

They got to his house in under five minutes. She wasn't really paying attention to the road. She was more interested in her chauffer. He was a natural behind the wheel and this late model Italian supercar was perfect for him. Sure, it wasn't exactly roomy inside for his big frame, but he worked the gears and sped down the dark streets with a quiet confidence she admired.

When they got to his place, he pulled all the way down the drive beside the house and into the backyard. There was a large garage back there she hadn't noticed before. She'd want to investigate what other little surprises he had locked away in there later, but for now, the pool was calling her name.

They took a different path to the pool area and it was clear someone had been there before them. Whoever it was had already turned on the soft lights and there was a bottle of wine in an ice bucket along with two crystal goblets on the patio table. Steve had thought of everything, apparently. And planned ahead.

She stripped as she walked toward the pool, her thoughts

on feeling the invigorating, life-giving water against her skin as soon as possible. And then, as soon after that as she could manage, she wanted to feel Steve's hard muscled body against her, both of them surrounded by the water while he took her places only he was able to take her.

Yeah, that sounded like the perfect way to spend the rest of the evening. The wine could wait.

She stripped off and dove into the deep end of the pool without waiting for him. She felt the water close around her, welcoming her, seeping into every sense and giving her new energy. After the events of the past few days, she needed all she could get of its buoyant support.

She began to swim a bit, loosening the tightness in her muscles and relaxing in her favorite environment. A few minutes later, she felt rather than heard Steve enter the water. The liquid communicated his presence to her, knowing her joy in welcoming her mate. She broke the surface and breathed deeply. She must've been under longer than she'd thought. Sometimes, it was easy to lose track of time when she was completely immersed.

Trisha saw Steve gliding under the surface, straight for her. Taking a deep breath, she sank once more to meet him.

He reached for her, encircling her with his strong arms, and she met him in kind, wrapping herself around him much as the water encircled them both. They rose together to the surface this time, kissing as they broke through from the underwater world she loved into the air-filled world in which she lived.

The kiss went on and on as the water supported them. The lower halves of their bodies slid against each other and she was gratified to learn that he too was naked. And ready for her. She smiled against his mouth. She loved how he was always ready for her, no matter what had come before.

"What's so funny?" he asked, pulling back a little to look into her eyes.

"Not funny. Fantastic," she corrected him. "I love how you feel against me. I love even more how you feel inside me."

"Talk like that will get you in trouble," he warned with a low growl and teasing smile. The sound and the expression on his handsome face turned her on like nobody's business. "I think I like your kind of trouble. In fact, I think I'm addicted to it."

She dipped her head and kissed him again, taking him down with her into the deeps for a moment out of time. She was very aware he couldn't breathe the way she could. He wouldn't be able to stay underwater as long. But she'd look out for him. She'd have him back in the air before anything bad could happen to spoil the mood.

She released him and swam, giving him the option of rising for air. He didn't. He followed immediately and she realized she'd underestimated him a bit. He could hold his breath a little longer than she'd thought. A little longer than most humans, but then she should have expected that. Being a shifter, he was exceptional in every way.

She swam to the shallow end and took a seat on the steps, half-in and half-out of the water. The night air on her wet body made her nipples pucker. She saw the way his gaze honed in on her breasts as he rose out of the water like some kind of sea god.

He really was amazing. Her own personal Poseidon come to give her anything she wanted.

And what she wanted most at the moment was him.

She spread her legs, inviting him to take his place between them, and he obliged. She smiled, but his face was hard as granite, his expression hard to read.

"Something wrong?"

"No, not for a shifter. But I have to be honest with you. You were raised human and you might feel differently once you know."

"Once I know what?" She was growing concerned. He seemed so serious. Almost nervous about what he had to say to her.

"I feel it's only right to tell you, we're not alone."

He pointed above her head and she craned her neck to look back, fearing his brothers or somebody else was watching, but all she saw was a big owl perched on the peak of his roof. And then she realized. The owl was, in all likelihood, a shifter.

But it looked like an owl. Her confused mind didn't know what to make of its presence.

"Who is that?"

"One of my men. A guy I've known for a long time. He's guarding us overnight, along with a few others, but he's the only one who can see us right now." Steve drew closer, coming down over her, shielding her with his body.

She hadn't bothered to cover up. The owl was behind her and didn't have a good angle to see much of her at the moment. Though she realized he'd probably gotten an eyeful when she'd walked into the backyard and stripped as she went.

"Nudity—even having sex—in front of others isn't that big a deal for shifters. We have to strip to shift, so we get used to seeing each other in the buff in our teens when most of us begin to shift. It's not that big a deal."

"But if we continue..." She couldn't quite put the scandalous thoughts she was having into words.

"If we continue, he'll watch. And he'll probably get off on it. Horny devil that he is," Steve muttered, shooting the owl a disgusted, yet amused look.

It was clear to her that Steve didn't mind the other man watching. In fact, she started to think about it and realized she wasn't all that upset by the idea either. In fact, it was even a little...arousing.

*Oh, wow.* The thought of being watched made her tummy clench and sent little sparks of heat coursing through her veins. Dare she?

One more look over her shoulder and she took a leap. She was living among shifters now. She was going to be learning and trying all sorts of new things. Steve had already shown her so much. She trusted him to guide her through all the discoveries she was going to make. As she would guide him through the things he would learn about her magic and abilities. They were a team. They were in this together.

And if occasionally they had a voyeur...well, that might just add a little spice to things. She'd at least give it a chance. Her body was on board with the idea, her senses lighting up like a Christmas tree at the thought of fucking in front of a stranger.

Well, not a stranger. Somebody Steve knew. A shapeshifter. An owl. A soldier and hunter. One of Steve's *men*, he'd said. So he must be a tough guy. She liked that idea.

Trisha turned back to Steve and snaked her hand up around his neck to pull him down to meet her kiss. That was all the answer he needed. Her excitement ratcheted up another notch when he lowered himself over her, gliding through the water until there was nothing between them. He slid inside easily, beginning to rock even as the water supported them both, the rhythmic waves pushing them toward completion even as her body strained toward his.

*Oh, yes.* This was what she'd wanted. Her man. Her mate. The moon, the stars, the night wind, the welcoming water...and a watcher adding a new spice to the mix.

She didn't look at the owl again, but she knew he was there. Just knowing that made her senses fly higher, her body pushing toward a new pinnacle. She hadn't thought she could get any hotter, but when Steve lowered his lips to her breasts, pushing her back to half-lie on the tile behind her, exposing her to view from above...well...she exploded.

The sensation rocketed through her, only to be replaced a moment later by another explosion. This one augmenting and surpassing the last. His lips tugged at her breasts as his cock pumped into her in strong beats, pounding now, claiming, driving her toward yet another climax.

She opened her eyes and saw the moon and stars above them. And the owl. His piercing topaz gaze met hers and held. She saw the intelligence there. Knew somehow that even in his owl form, the male behind those eyes was aroused, watching her, turned on by the passion between her and her mate.

Just knowing he was up there added a little extra edge she never would have expected. Trisha had never considered herself very adventurous sexually, but with Steve, she wanted to try it all. She wanted to do anything and everything for him...to him. He'd given her the confidence in herself to try just about anything.

"Come for me now," he whispered urgently near her ear, and her body answered the call, meeting his passion with her own and sending her straight up to the moon with pleasure.

Her soul danced with his among the stars for a short moment...an eternity. The two of them entwined. Mated. Together forever.

And then the long fall back to earth...and water, through the air while the fire of spent passion ebbed inside them. They were elemental. They were timeless. Together.

The next morning, they woke before dawn, making love urgently, as if they hadn't spent most of the night entwined, lost in each other. Each time was fresh and new. Vital.

They snuck out before the dawn kissed the sky, heading back toward the Pack house so they could have breakfast with the girls and preserve the falsehood that they were merely interested in each other. Not already mated. Not fucking like bunnies at every opportunity.

They were in a large, dark blue SUV this morning. He'd unlocked his giant garage and given her the nickel tour in the semi-darkness. He'd pointed out the sexy Italian beast he'd driven her here in last night, as well as a souped-up muscle car straight from Detroit's heyday. There was a giant motorcycle and a few other surprises as well, but he'd chosen the SUV for the day's work.

"I've arranged for the helicopter tour today." They chatted as he drove them competently back to the Pack house. There was a car in front and one behind, but they weren't very obvious. The approach to guarding their route was more casual since the showdown on the Strip.

"That's awesome. Thank you for doing it." She knew her friends were going to love it. "To be honest, though, I'm a little nervous. I've never been in a helicopter before."

He reached over and took her hand. "You'll love it. I promise. Do you trust me?"

"Of course." She didn't even have to think about her answer.

"Then trust me to fly you all safely around. I've done it a dozen times for visiting business contacts. We're using the big chopper today. It's a lot like the one they ferry the president around in back east. Big and roomy inside with all the amenities. There's even a wet bar."

"You're kidding."

He looked over and winked at her. His smile was as charming as ever and it took her breath away, like always. Would she ever get used to how good looking her mate was? Maybe in a century or two.

"I never kid." His mock seriousness made her laugh and he joined in. A moment later, he pulled up in front of the Pack house and they snuck in before the sun rose.

# CHAPTER ELEVEN

She knew her friends hadn't seen her walk of shame—sneaking back into the Pack house—when they all convened for breakfast an hour or two later. She'd taken a shower in one of the guest rooms on the floor where all the girls were housed, making it her own. Steve had left just enough of her luggage to make it look like she was sleeping there and she dutifully disarranged the sheets on the bed to continue the ruse, just in case any of her friends came knocking.

One by one, they woke and got ready. Trisha went around, knocking on doors, acting as hall mother for the morning, telling them what time to meet for breakfast. They all converged in the hallway about the same time and walked downstairs as a group.

Steve met them at the foot of the stairs, making a show of wishing them all a good morning and then leading them to the dining room. A few of the girls stopped dead in their tracks when they got a look at the handsome men and equally stunning women who were already seated around the big room in various stages of breaking their fast. There were really only a few werewolves there, but they sure did make an impression.

Trisha recognized a few faces from that first night. Sure enough, the big guy who'd been flirting with Molly at the bar came across the room to meet them. He smiled at Molly and Trisha saw the way her shy friend's pale features flamed with a betraying blush even as she smiled back at him. There was definitely some mutual attraction going on there.

"Some of you may remember Jed from the other night. He and his friends were chatting with you when the problems started at that bar." Steve frowned and some of the girls looked away from the handsome werewolf to listen to Steve. The rest seemed fixated on the good-looking young men all around them. "He helped bring you all here."

"Thank you, Mr. uh…" Molly uncharacteristically stepped forward to offer her hand. The big werewolf took her small hand in his and smiled at her. Molly just about swooned, but Trisha understood. The man made an impact, even when his charm wasn't aimed directly at you.

"Robinson. But please, call me Jed. You're Molly, right?" He asked as if he already knew the answer and Trisha saw the way Molly reacted to the fact that the hunkalicious werewolf remembered her name.

Sadly, Molly was usually forgotten among the rest of the girls because she was the shyest of them all. She wasn't bad looking, but she didn't really dress to bring out her best features, and her quiet nature sometimes got overwhelmed by some of the more forceful personalities in their little group. It was good to see her basking in the attention of a handsome man. She seemed to blossom before their eyes and it gave Trisha a warm feeling to see her friend so happy.

Jed took Molly's hand and led her, and by default the rest of the gang, toward a long table. They had come downstairs ready to go, so everyone dumped their purses and bags on chairs and went to sample the buffet. Molly was escorted everywhere by Jed and he didn't seem to want to let her out of his reach.

"You think maybe something's going on there?" Trisha whispered to Steve when he came up beside her at the end of the food line. She nodded toward Molly and her admirer.

"Could be. He's definitely interested and I've never really

seen him so intense in his pursuit of a human before." Steve watched the couple as he seemed to consider the werewolf's body language. "I wonder if Little Miss Muffet is ready to handle the Big Bad Wolf?"

"I think you're mixing up your fairytales. It's Little Red Riding Hood and the Big Bad Wolf." She chuckled and handed him one of the plates that were stacked at the end of the table. Steve shrugged and gave her a set of silverware wrapped in a cloth napkin. It was then that she noticed the fineness of the china and the quality of the table linens. "Do you guys always go this fancy for meals, or is this special for my friends' benefit?"

Steve looked around and shrugged again. "I don't eat here all that often, but I think this is pretty standard for the Pack house. We make a lot of money building things. Why not enjoy it?"

Trisha considered his words and realized he was right. She also realized that Redstone Construction probably paid their employees *really* well. The sheer amount and variety of food available surprised her. It was a banquet fit for a king and the quantities the werewolves were putting on their plates was kind of amazing. Steve too, when it came his turn, filled the big plate with heaping helpings of eggs, meat and only a little toast on the side. No doubt about it. He was definitely a carnivore.

Trisha took a much smaller portion, as did her friends, who mostly went for the fruits and bread selections. When they got back to the table, some newcomers were already there. One was seated right next to Trisha and she wasn't too surprised to find it was her brother. The human one. Deke.

"So you're staying then?" She went on the attack rather than wait for his disapproval. She knew Deke wasn't happy about her hooking up with his friend, but he was going to have to learn to live with it.

"Dad thought it would be best if one of us stuck with your group, just in case. Plus…" He paused uncharacteristically. "I owe you both an apology. I'm sorry, sis. Sorry, man." He held out his hand for Steve to shake and the two men nodded at each other very seriously. Deke looked around to make sure nobody was eavesdropping as he pitched his voice a little lower. "I had a long talk with Grif about shifters and cougars in particular. If even half what he said is true—and I've never doubted Grif's word on anything—then Red is going to make you very happy. And if you're happy, I'm happy, Trish. I just wanted the best for you and it took some convincing—particularly because I didn't know the full story about who or what you were, Red—but I'm convinced now and I wish you both nothing but the best."

Trisha leaned in and hugged her big brother, emotion choking her throat for a moment. Instead, she hugged him tight, feeling the safety of his arms the way she had since she was a little girl. Only, she had grown up now. She could take care of herself for the most part. And anything she couldn't handle, she now had Steve to rely on.

Their relationship as siblings would change from here on out, but it was good to know that they would have a relationship. A good one from all indications. She sent a prayer of thanks up to the Goddess for helping Deke understand.

"I love you, Deke."

"I love you too, Squirt." He rocked her from side-to-side once more before letting her go. She stood away and realized everyone at the table was looking at them.

"Hey, guys." She managed to control her blush at being the center of attention, caught in an emotional moment. "Do you all know my big brother Deke?"

She was saved further embarrassment by the need to make a few introductions, and by the time everyone had met everyone else, they were all seated and digging into their breakfasts. Steve had introduced Jeremy Newmar, who Trisha knew was the son of the Pack Alpha. He'd helped get them to the Pack house that terrible night they'd been drugged, but he acted as if he'd never seen them before, knowing none of the women—except Lynda, who was keeping mum—would recognize him. They'd all been unconscious before he'd helped carry them into the house.

Jed introduced a few more of the guys who'd been flirting with her friends at the bar and she was glad to finally put names with the faces. One was Jed's brother, Paul. Another was a friend who worked on the same crew, he said. She assumed he meant a work crew of some kind since they all worked for Redstone Construction.

After a leisurely breakfast at which she ate entirely too much, Trisha and the rest of the gang—including her brother and Jed—piled into SUVs and were driven to a helipad behind the Redstone Construction headquarters building. As they pulled around the edge of the building, she saw the giant helicopter waiting for them.

It was way larger than anything she'd expected. She'd been wondering how all of them were going to fit inside a single helicopter, but when she saw this behemoth, she didn't have to wonder. It would fit a small army inside.

She walked toward it with the rest of them but Steve tugged her toward the front. She didn't understand why at first, but then she realized he was going to fly the big machine. And Deke was already strapping into the co-pilot's seat.

When Steve had asked if she trusted him to fly her and her friends around, she hadn't realized he actually meant he'd be the one flying the helicopter. And she'd had no idea her big brother knew how to fly one of these things. Yet Deke looked very competent going through the pre-flight checklist. As if he'd done this a million times before.

"Is this a military helicopter?"

Steve grinned. "It does have some similarity to a certain troop transport your brother and I might have piloted in places we can't mention." He had that cat-who-swallowed-the-canary look on his face that made her want to laugh.

Oh yeah, boys and their toys. Steve was like her brothers in that respect. He clearly loved getting the chance to operate the big machine again.

He gave her a headset and then showed her how to flip the channels so she could talk to him—and Deke—privately. The pilots were on a different channel than the passengers, but he wanted her to be able to talk to him if she wanted. She liked his thoughtfulness.

He also gave her the seat nearest the cockpit so she could look out the front as well as the side windows if she wished. Everybody else arranged themselves around the cabin and Jed even acted as bartender, making drinks at the wet bar while Deke and Steve went through their checks prior to takeoff.

By the time they were airborne, Trisha's nerves were calmed. Steve and Deke wouldn't let them fall out of the sky. They were battle tested and competent. She trusted both of them with her life.

That thought firmly in mind, she began to look out the windows, enjoying the novel view. Jed acted as an impromptu tour guide, pointing out different features as they flew past. The girls were really enjoying themselves, and before she even realized it, a couple of hours had passed. Steve surprised them by bringing the helicopter in for a landing in the middle of a small stretch of green in the desert. It was an oasis of sorts. And she could easily see the resort that had been built around it.

The guys were securing the helicopter while everyone took off their headsets. The noise from the propellers was dissipating enough to be able to speak and hear without the help of the headsets.

"Time for lunch," Jed announced, much to the delight of the women in the group. They'd gotten a late start after lingering over breakfast and it was definitely lunch time.

"You planned this?" Trisha looked at Steve, smiling as he shrugged.

"It's not often we get to treat a group of ladies to a pleasant afternoon. I figured this would make the party memorable after the bad start you all had. Make some good memories to replace the bad."

She reached up and kissed him, not caring who saw.

"You're terrific." And she meant it. What a great guy. She laid one on him even as he smiled at her words.

A wolf whistle broke them apart a moment later and she realized she'd sort of forgotten they were in the middle of a helipad surrounded by her friends. Trisha blushed a bit. She could feel the heat of it in her cheeks, but she didn't move away from Steve. No. She was staking her claim on him and it felt good.

They walked up the path to the resort to find a private room waiting for them. This time, the resort's efficient staff waited on them hand and foot as they consumed a lovely luncheon. Steve had been right. The girls would remember this luxury as a highlight of the trip. Especially Molly, who was being looked after by the big werewolf who seemed very, *very* interested in her.

On the way back, the helicopter rocked a bit unexpectedly. Trisha looked forward into the cockpit and hastily turned the controls on the headset so she could hear what Steve and her brother were talking about.

"—definitely shooting at us," she heard Deke say. "Sniper nest on that rise over there."

She squinted, but try as she might, she couldn't see what her brother pointed to. Then again, she didn't really know what she was looking for.

"Buzz low over him. I'm jumping out. Circle around and pick me up only if it's safe. Otherwise, I'll leg it back after I deal with him." Steve was already unbuttoning his shirt and leaving some of his possessions behind. She took that to mean he intended to shapeshift.

The big helicopter had a passenger door on the side of the main cabin, where they'd boarded, but now she could see there were access doors on either side of the cockpit. She didn't know if such a thing was standard equipment or maybe something the Redstones had added to their chopper, but it was clear Steve intended to use the hinged panel right next to him to take a nosedive out of a perfectly good helicopter.

Her friends didn't seem to think anything was wrong,

looking out the windows and enjoying the view. Only Trisha had access to the pilots' channel on her headset and only she knew exactly what was going on. The others probably just thought they'd hit a bit of turbulence or something when the chopper bounced again.

Deke was in control of the craft while Steve unlatched the locks on the door panel. He really was going to do it. Trisha's heart beat fast, her pulse nearly choking her with anxiety. Was he crazy? She had to stop him.

"Don't you dare jump!" she shouted over the pilots' channel. Deke winced, but Steve turned to her with a serious expression.

"Honey, this is what I do. I can't let someone shoot at you without at least *trying* to rip him to shreds. I'll do anything it takes to keep you safe, and right now someone is shooting at this helicopter."

"Shooting?" She was alarmed. She hadn't seen any shots.

"It's bullet proof, Trish," Deke told her. Including the glass. See?" He pointed to a star-like pattern in the glass next to him and she realized it had been made by a bullet. She sucked in a breath.

"You could have been killed!" For a minute, fear threatened to overwhelm her.

"Nah, Squirt. Bullet proof, remember?" He had the nerve to smile at her. She wanted to shake him. "But this definitely means we didn't get them all on the Strip. There's at least one that I can see and he's shooting at us. Because of our flight pattern and the sightseeing we're doing, we have to go over him again, so we might as well take the opportunity to take him out. Don't worry about Red. He could do this in his sleep."

"I'm touched that you're worried about me, sweetheart," Steve added. "But really, I have to do this. Deke can fly you to safety and Jed is a qualified pilot as well. You'll be okay. Just trust me to do this. I can't leave a threat to you out there running around free to shoot at us any old time."

He smiled at her and she knew she had to let him go. It

might be the hardest thing she'd ever had to do, but she knew she couldn't interfere and make him deny his instincts and training.

"You be smart and come back to me in one piece, Redstone. Do you hear me?" She was fighting tears, but she had to be strong.

He smiled and winked. "I will always come back to you, love."

A moment later, Deke swooped downward with the helicopter and Steve jumped. She tried to watch where he'd gone, but they were moving too fast.

"What's happening?"

"It's cool," Deke said, moving the chopper around so he could get a better vantage. "He landed right on the guy. Didn't even have to go furry or anything. He's got the man and is tying him up. Just one shooter."

A tug on her sleeve made Trisha look back into the cabin where the rest of her friends were watching her with varying degrees of alarm and concern. She hastily switched the headset back to their frequency.

It was Marcia who spoke first.

"Did your boyfriend just jump out of the helicopter?"

Hearing it put that way, in such an outraged tone made Trisha laugh. She was close to hysterics, but she had to remain strong.

"Somebody was shooting at us," she explained. "Red is just taking care of the problem." She couldn't believe that was her voice. She sounded so calm when she was really anything but.

The women started talking excitedly, but she switched back to the pilot frequency to talk to her brother.

"Red's going to use the prisoner's vehicle to transport them both back to base," Deke reported. "It's under control."

"You're just going to leave him there?" She was outraged.

"He's got backup on the way and the prisoner is secure. The guy wet his pants when he saw Red jump out of the helicopter." She heard the amusement in her brother's voice, but she didn't think it was funny at all. Not when they were leaving Steve alone in the desert with someone who had been trying to kill them all.

They argued some more, but eventually Deke brought them safely back to Redstone Construction headquarters. Everyone was still talking excitedly about what Steve had done, and Trisha bit her lip and worried, waiting for Steve. She needed to see him in person, to know he was all right.

They'd been ushered into a conference room where refreshments were waiting. Nobody was going anywhere until they figured out who had been shooting and why. Trisha paced by the window, watching the road until she saw him.

She rushed out of the conference room toward the front doors. She flew into his arms the moment he stepped into the building. She'd been *so* worried.

She knew she was trembling, but she couldn't help it. Steve soothed her, stroking her hair and holding her body close to his, offering his comfort and strength. She honestly didn't know what she'd have done if something had happened to him.

"Hey, Red, what's the sit rep?"

Trisha heard her brother's voice from behind her and she could have cursed him for his bad timing. She'd just needed another moment in her lover's arms. Then maybe she could let him go easily. As it was, she had to drag herself away from his embrace to turn and find Deke wasn't the only one watching them, waiting to learn what Steve had to say.

"Come on, love. Everybody needs to hear this." Steve took her elbow and ushered her into the big conference room.

Everyone sat, stood or perched around the room according to their moods, waiting to hear Steve's report. He didn't make them wait long.

"Turns out our gunman was a last minute hire. One of your father's business rivals recognized you at the resort where we went for lunch, Marcia, and he put in a call to this local man who does contract killing. Your dad has some enemies who want to hurt him by hurting his family."

"Seriously?" Trisha felt compelled to ask. After all the magical stuff that had happened up to this point, it seemed almost anticlimactic that this gunman was of the ordinary hit man variety.

"Seriously," Steve answered, giving her a nod. Yeah, he was just a normal hit man. If such a person could be described as *normal.*

"Wow." Marcia flopped back in her seat. "I mean, I knew he had enemies, but this is just…"

Some of the other girls began to comfort Marcia, who seemed to be really shaken by Steve's news. The mood was subdued as they made their way back to the Pack house. Going out on the town was out of the question tonight. Nobody felt like it to start with, and it just wasn't safe.

The girls ate dinner in the Pack house dining room, joined by Jed, Paul, Jeremy and a few other werewolves. Conversation ranged far and wide until Marcia suggested she call her father and cut their trip short. She wanted to leave tomorrow and most of the girls agreed.

Molly went along with the group but Trisha could see she really wanted to stay and explore the budding romance between herself and the big werewolf. Well, if it was real, they'd probably get their chance at some point. It wasn't like Molly didn't have ties to the Redstones now. She was one of Trisha's closest friends and Trisha was marrying into the Clan. Molly would probably see Jed again sooner or later.

They spent a quiet evening among the werewolves, though only Lynda and Trisha knew the true nature of their hosts. Lynda was in deep conversation with the Alpha and his wife, studiously ignoring Deke and his attempts to talk to her. Trisha knew her brother had always had a thing for Lynda, but she'd never returned his interest. It made Trisha feel sad for her brother, but now that she knew Lynda was a magical half-fey being, she was almost glad Deke's advances had been rejected. She didn't want to see him hurt even worse by a fickle fey.

When everyone started to go up to bed one by one, Trisha turned to Steve.

"Better stay here tonight," he answered her unspoken question so quietly that only she could hear him. "Go on up and I'll join you when the coast is clear." He winked at her and she gave him a peck on the cheek before excusing herself and going to her assigned bedroom.

When Steve snuck in a few minutes later, she was primed and ready for him. It seemed she was always ready for him, but in this case, anticipation had heightened her awareness to a fever pitch.

"It occurs to me that if your bachelorette party hadn't been interrupted, you girls might have gotten up to all sorts of naughtiness. Am I right?"

"Maybe." She played coy. Her cat was in a mischievous mood and she was eager to find where it would lead.

"What was on the agenda? Come on, you can be honest with me. I'm sure it wasn't anything too bad." His smile dared her as he leaned against the door, his hand on the knob, fingers turning the lock back and forth, back and forth. Was he going to lock it? Or leave it open so that anyone might be able to just walk in on them?

"Well, we had tickets to see some of the shows," she temporized.

"What kind of shows?" He pounced verbally when she didn't go into detail. "Was there, by chance, a ticket in your portfolio for a strip club? That seems pretty standard fare for bachelor and bachelorette parties."

"There might have been something like that on our itinerary," she admitted, the mood in the room decidedly playful.

"Well, then…" He straightened and she noticed that the door was definitely *un*locked. "I'm sorry you had to miss such an evening's entertainment. I'm glad though too. I wouldn't want you ogling any other men. Not now that I've claimed you as mine." He said it as if he had every right to say such barbaric—thrilling—things. And maybe he did, she realized. She certainly felt possessive about him.

"That goes both ways, you know," she warned him.

"Agreed," he said immediately, stilling her heart. "My days of roaming are behind me now. Thank the Goddess." He advanced another pace into the room. "But that doesn't mean I still wouldn't like to see a strip show. A very special strip show with only one stripper. You."

Her breath caught. And then her own playful side came out. "That also goes both ways. You strip for me and I'll return the favor."

"Ladies first?" He gave her an almost boyish, appealing look. She laughed.

"Nice try. But I'm the one who missed out on the floor show. I think maybe you should make that up to me. Then, if you do a good job, I'll do it for you."

"Oh, you do it for me, all right," he agreed. "But I think I like this game. Sit back and prepare to be entertained."

Giggling, Trisha sat on the bed, switching on the clock radio on the night stand. She tapped a few of the preset buttons until she landed on a song with a sexy groove. She turned it up a little and waited.

Sure enough, Steve's lean hips began to sway. He had the sinuous grace of the cat that shared his soul as he began undressing, one item at a time. He stalked slowly across the floor toward her, holding her gaze as he bared his skin, swaying in time with the music. He wasn't really dancing, but she didn't care. This was the hottest thing a man had ever done for her. And Steve was better than any *man* she'd ever been with. Probably because he wasn't really a man. Not entirely, at least.

His animal nature showed in the way he moved, the way he focused on her as if he was going to pounce and then eat her up. She hoped there would be some *eating* involved, but not the painful kind. She wanted his mouth on her skin. Everywhere. Just as she wanted to devour him. She wanted to

BIANCA D'ARC

suck him and make him come in her mouth. She wanted it all with him. Only him.

He tore his shirt off over his head and swung it around on the tip of his finger a few times before tossing it aside. It landed on the other side of the room, but she didn't care. She was too busy salivating over his chest and the sleek muscles that rippled every time he moved. He saw the direction of her gaze and flexed a few times, posing almost comically for her like a muscle man would do.

But she wasn't laughing. Oh, no. Her lady parts were quivering along with his every flex. *Damn, he was fine.* Quite possibly the most amazingly fit man she'd ever seen. There was grace and power in his every move, and if she turned on her imagination, it wasn't hard to see the slithering gait of the cougar in his sexy walk as he came toward her again, his hands unbuttoning the buttons on his pants.

*Oh, boy. Was it getting hot in here?*

He lowered the pants—no underwear—an inch at a time. And there were a lot of inches to uncover. He kept walking, his hard cock bobbing slowly in time with his movements as he released it from his pants until he stood in front of her. He nudged her knees apart until he stood between them. She was perched on the edge of the bed, his cock in line with her mouth.

It seemed only natural to reach out and lick him.

He groaned and she felt the need to hear that sound again. She lifted her hands, one to fondle his balls, the other to wrap around the base of his cock as she guided it into her mouth. She knew a moment of triumph when he groaned again, louder this time, as she sucked and played with him.

He pushed her away before he could come, rubbing her cheeks and hair with his hardness before he stepped back. He flopped onto the bed next to her, propping himself on his elbows as he looked at her.

"Your turn, sexy." His smile invited her to kiss him, which she did before climbing to her unsteady feet.

She fiddled with the radio for a moment, finding a song

170

she could dance to and then she began to sway, working her way into the song and the proper frame of mind. She'd never stripped for anyone before, but she knew she was a good dancer. She could do this. In fact, she really *wanted* to do this.

Steve made her feel like a sex goddess. Nobody had ever made her feel that way before and it was empowering. Enlightening.

She moved, swiveling her hips in what she hoped was a sinuous move. Judging by the look in Steve's eyes, she was doing okay. She slid her top off over her head, moving it a few inches at a time, slowly, as sensuously as possible. She repeated his little twirl of fabric before tossing it in the opposite direction of where his shirt had gone earlier.

Steve's gaze was focused on her breasts, spilling out over the top of her push-up bra when she bent over to rid herself of her pants. Those too, went sailing over the floor to another part of the big room. And then she was in her underwear. A matching set, thank goodness. She'd packed new stuff for the trip, not liking to have old, mismatched pieces when she was on vacation.

She tried her best to make the awkward, reaching-behind-her-back move to unhook her bra look sexy, but she was afraid she'd failed when Steve motioned her over. He crooked his finger and she went to him like a slave being ordered around by her master. Now that was a fantasy she'd like to try with him...later. For now, she was the stripper. Yet another of her fantasies come to life with, and for, this incredible man.

Using his finger again, making a circular motion in the air, he instructed her to turn so that her back was to him. She almost jumped when he touched her, his hands sliding over her ass and up her spine to the catch on her bra. He unhooked it easily and backed away to recline on the bed once more as she stood in front of him between his spread knees. His cock was standing at attention and he stuffed some pillows behind his back as she turned. That freed up his hands and one immediately went to his cock, grasping and rubbing as he watched her.

She licked her lips and saw the way his muscles tightened. Good. He was hot and hard. Ready and waiting. But she had to finish the show first.

Slowly, she lowered the straps of her bra, one at a time, turning and teasing him, jiggling and bouncing as much as she could manage without dislodging the cups altogether. She was built on the big side, which she thought he liked judging from his rapt attention. All the men she'd been with—precious few that there had been—had liked her breasts. Steve seemed no exception.

Trisha lowered the straps and then, one by one, allowed the cups to slip free, baring her nipples to the night air. They immediately went hard—both from the air and from Steve's laser-like gaze following their every motion.

She let the bra fall to the floor, raised her arms over her head and gave him an eyeful as she moved to the music. Her breasts swayed with her, bouncing in time with her movements. And then she couldn't take it anymore, she moved her hands downward, between her legs, rubbing and then retreating. Taking the thin fabric of her panties in her fingers, she slid them down over each hip, turning to shake her ass in Steve's direction. He seemed to appreciate it, if the way he squeezed his cock was any indication.

And then he growled. And pounced.

In one move, he sat up and moved his hands over hers on the sides of her panties. He moved them downward and the silky fabric slid off her ass and slithered down her legs. She stepped out of the leg holes when they landed on the floor and followed Steve's guiding hands on her hips, turning to face him.

He lowered his head, biting her small belly with playful nips as he moved his hands around to cup her ass, the fingers delving between her cheeks and downward. One found her anus and pushed a little bit inside as she squeaked. Nobody had ever done that to her before. If asked, she would have thought it wouldn't feel good at all, but she surprised herself by pushing back to make him go a little deeper.

Then he slid his other hand into the slick wetness between her thighs and pushed inward. Big, blunt fingers swirled around her clit for a moment, making her knees tremble before he pushed two thick digits up into her opening. That surprising penetration, coupled with the pressure behind made her shout as a small climax hit her, almost making her knees buckle. As it was, she reached out to support herself, grabbing for his shoulders to keep her upright.

He held her throughout, kissing her skin, nibbling on the places he could reach.

When she had a reasonable amount of control over her body again, she pushed at his shoulders, pushing him back onto the bed. He complied, a questioning smile hovering around his lips. He didn't have long to wait to see what she had in mind as she climbed over him, both of them scooting farther back on the big bed for stability. She reached between them and guided his ready cock into her wet opening.

Almost triumphantly, she sat on him, taking him deep, loving the feel of him filling her, taking her, making them one for this brief moment out of time. She couldn't savor it though. She had to move. The passion riding her made it imperative that she begin moving almost immediately.

His hands went to her hips, guiding and helping as best he could while she jumped his bones. Her movements grew erratic as her climax hit and he flipped them over and began a pounding rhythm of his own that drove her even higher. She became one long, never-ending, orgasm of pleasure as he claimed her body, pushing into her with more force than she'd been able to manage in the other position. She loved every minute of it. And when she cried out, it was his name on her lips.

His groan followed a moment later, her name sounding sweet when he said it in just that tone of total and complete ecstasy.

A knock on the bedroom door woke Trisha from a sound

sleep. She was snuggled in Steve's arms when reality hit and she realized where they were and who was likely knocking on the door. Her eyes widened in panic. One of her friends was out there and would likely barge in if she didn't answer the door.

And then the jig would be up. They'd know she was sleeping with Steve, which wasn't exactly in character for her. She'd never jumped into a physical relationship with a man so fast. Her friends would be surprised. And probably concerned.

Not to mention they'd tease her mercilessly.

The knock sounded again and Trisha scrambled out of bed, searching helplessly for her robe. She finally snagged it near the foot of the bed. She had laid it out on top of the comforter yesterday but hadn't worn it and it had slid to the floor in a silky heap.

It took her a moment to sort out where the arm holes were and struggle into the difficult piece of fabric. She hopped toward the door, dodging other bits of their clothing that had ended up strewn all over the room. By the time she reached the door, the handle was beginning to turn. One of her friends was getting impatient. Dammit.

Trisha took hold of the slowly turning door handle and opened it, peeking through a small crack in the doorway.

"What's up?" Trisha asked, well aware that her voice was scratchy with sleep. She blinked a few times at the light coming in through the window in the hall. It was later in the morning than she'd thought.

"You slept late, so I thought I'd give you a wakeup call. My father is sending the jet to take us home, so we need to leave in a couple of hours. Everyone else is already downstairs, eating breakfast." Marcia looked suspicious, trying to get a look behind Trisha into the room. "Do you have company?" Marcia's voice dropped to a conspiratorial whisper as she grinned.

Caught, Trisha felt her cheeks heat with a blush. Damn her fair skin.

Marcia's eyebrows rose as her grin turned into a full-out smile. "Well, good for you. Is it that hunky Steve? He was all over you yesterday. Is he as good as he looks?"

Trisha knew Steve could probably hear every whispered word with his shifter ears. "Yes and yes. Now give me a few minutes and I'll join you downstairs for breakfast."

Marcia backed away, giving Trisha an exaggerated thumbs up as Trisha closed the door and turned the little lock for good measure.

"Busted." Steve's amused voice came to her from the bed. After the light in the hallway, she couldn't see too well. They'd closed all the curtains in this room and they were thick fabric that hid most of the light.

She sighed. "Yeah. This is going to be fun. Half of them will be high fiving me and the other half will be asking if I'm sure about all this."

Steve stood and came over to her to take her in his arms. He was so warm. So strong. So comforting as he rocked her from side-to-side, hugging her, offering so much support without even being asked. He was a very tactile man, always touching her, stroking her skin, hugging her. She liked it. A lot.

"Don't get on the plane. Stay with me," he whispered, and she was so very tempted.

"I want to, but I have to face the music at home and get some things settled with my friends and family. But..." she looked up at his face, all shadows and angles in the uncertain light, "you could come with me."

His lips widened in a smile and he bent his head to align their lips so he could place a tender kiss on her mouth. "Are you taking me home to meet Mama?"

"Something like that," she agreed. "But don't worry. She's going to love you. Because you love me."

# EPILOGUE

As it turned out, Steve hit it off with Mrs. Morrow, who insisted on calling him Steven, much to his amusement. She was a dynamic woman who reminded him a little bit of his own mother, though she wasn't a shifter, of course. For all intents and purposes, she was human, though Slade had confided that Deke probably had some mage blood in his lineage, though it was dormant. Whether that affinity for magic came from his late father or his mother, Steve didn't know. That wasn't one of his talents. At some point, Slade or his mate would meet Mrs. Morrow and be able to tell more, but it wasn't a high priority.

Steve loved Trisha. It was as simple as that. Whether or not she had mage blood in addition to the amazing gifts of her father's lineage didn't really matter to Steve. No, what mattered most was that she loved him too.

One thing that had surprised Steve was the sheer number of people watching the Morrow home. There was all kinds of surveillance going on and it made the hairs on the back of his neck stand on end to be watched so closely. He'd had a talk with the admiral about it when he'd first arrived, it had bothered him so much.

"You get used to it." Trisha's father had shrugged. "About half of them are on our side, watching the watchers. The rest are mostly agents of foreign powers trying to figure out what's going on with our Teams from my movements."

"It can't be easy living in a fishbowl. Especially with your abilities," Steve had observed.

"It's not, but if I'm to keep doing what I'm doing with the military at this level, then it's something I have to put up with."

"Uh, sir...?" Steve had an idea forming as he spoke. "Maybe not."

"What do you mean?" The admiral looked interested.

"Do you mind if I take a little stroll around the neighborhood? I have a few contacts in the area and it might just be feasible to call on some of them to help give you and your family a little more privacy."

"Supernatural help, you mean? What could shifters do for us?"

"More than shifters, sir. There are a few bloodletters who actually enjoy covert work, and several magic users that I know personally, in the area. One of them is practically a neighbor of yours. She lives a few miles away, but that's no distance at all to someone like her."

"A female?" The admiral looked skeptical, but then the Morrow men all seemed to have a blind spot when it came to women and their strengths.

"Let me talk to her and I'll see what she says. In any case, you should probably make her acquaintance. She's part of the local hierarchy. Very highly placed, in fact."

Steve didn't want to say more until he'd spoken to Sadie. She was one of his oldest friends and he meant that in every way possible. Sadie had been one of his mother's dear friends, for all that she was a witch. In that way—and many others— his mother had been very progressive. She judged a person on their own merits rather than allow stereotypes to interfere in her friendships.

Steve reconnoitered the area before visiting his mother's old friend. They spoke briefly and she seemed interested in learning more about the situation, which was a start. She agreed to look into the magical use in the area around the Morrow's home, and they would arrange a meeting to discuss strategy if she thought she could help. And payment. Witches didn't work for free. Even good witches like Sadie.

Steve also made it a point to invite Sadie to his wedding. Once Mrs. Morrow had gotten used to the idea of her only daughter getting married, she had jumped into wedding plans right away. Steve was given the guest room conveniently located in the pool house while Trisha stayed in her room in the main house.

There was no getting past her brothers for midnight rendezvous, which was annoying. Steve would've gone insane if they hadn't been able to sneak off together during the day to supposedly sightsee. The only sight he was really interested in seeing was his mate—naked and ready for him.

They managed to be together enough to calm the beast inside him, but he missed holding her at night while they slept. In only a few days, he'd gotten used to the feel of her in his arms, and now, sleeping alone, he knew something important was missing. Some*one* important. Vital, in fact.

Steve continued to work on the problem of all that surveillance and he went out to prowl at night a few times and ran across a few other shifters. Some of them, he knew. Redstone Construction had a big job site nearby and quite a few of the crew were people he had worked with in the past and knew well. He enlisted their help—once Sadie had laid a few preliminary spells on the area—to help clear out the *rodents*, as he liked to call them.

Without doing anything overt, between Sadie's magic and the shifter dirty tricks squad, they were able to cut the number of watchers by more than half in just a few nights. Life at the Morrow house was getting easier, but Steve had another idea in mind to help the family. His new family.

He took them on a tour of the housing development already under construction a few miles away on the outskirts of town. It was a Redstone site and it was one of the special ones. The moment they set foot on the site, they were on protected lands. Magically protected.

And everyone working there was a shifter or Other of some kind. It was okay to talk freely, which was something they couldn't do at the Morrow house, even now that the watchers had decreased in number.

"Redstone builds housing developments all the time," Steve explained as he took the family on a tour of the site. Several of the homes were complete. Several more were in various stages of completion and yet others had been sketched out with the land cleared enough to begin work. "But a few of our projects, scattered around the country at any given time, are extra special. This one, for example, is going to be a shifter neighborhood, built especially for Others and run by a Council of Alphas of the various Tribes, Packs and Clans that decide to take up residence. Right now, there's a small wolf Pack, a Pack of coyotes and several raptor Tribes that want to move in. We're building homes to suit each of them. See the balconies on that house over there?" Steve pointed to a three-story home with high balconies as well as roof access.

"Let me guess," Deke's tone was bored, but Steve knew he was thinking back to the shifters he'd met in Las Vegas. Deke had been especially fascinated by the birds. "The decks and railings offer perches to bird shifters."

Steve nodded. "The family who'll be moving in there has teenagers. They're just learning to fly, so they need different levels of relatively safe places to land. You'll notice all the trees in close proximity to the house in back. We left the old growth specifically so that they had cover and plenty of sturdy branches to learn to glide from." Steve pointed to another house as they walked down the street. "This one is for the local priestess. She's an older lady who can't handle stairs very well, so we built her a ranch-style house where everything is all on one floor. The bathroom has handrails and a special bathtub with a door so she can walk in without having to climb over the side of a conventional tub. She's a sweet old lady and we want to make life as easy as possible for her—as she makes our lives richer, serving the Goddess and our people."

"That's so sweet," Mrs. Morrow said, looking fondly at the ranch house. "It's good to see your people take such good care of others."

Steve let her words stand without comment, but he knew he was teaching the whole family about how shifter society worked. It was an important thing for them to know, since they would now be part of it to some extent. They'd be immersed in it if Steve had his way. But they didn't know that yet.

"You'll notice how we separated the raptors from the breeds that might want to hunt them. The priestess' house will act as a small buffer zone—and a reminder that we don't hunt each other in the neighborhood."

Mrs. Morrow looked at him, clearly shocked. "You *hunt* each other?"

Steve laughed. "Only for fun. The youngsters especially like to chase each other around—like kids playing tag. But it rarely turns dangerous. Only if there's instability or some kind of feud. But then the Alphas would step in and settle things. We all try to rub along together in peace as much as we can while not denying our animal natures. We're all hunters and we like to chase things. We rarely kill. Our human sides are able to control the desire. And our human sides like our food cooked for the most part." He grinned, inviting the others to laugh with him. They didn't really understand yet, but they would. Eventually.

He took them around a corner and soon they were looking at another part of the sprawling neighborhood. This was the part he really wanted to show them.

"The wolf Pack house will be on the next street and that whole area back there will be the Pack section. A few big cat families want homes in this area behind us, and this street will be where all the Alphas live—at the heart of the neighborhood, each on the edge of his own territory. They'll be neighbors and within close proximity to work out any issues between the different groups."

"Sounds like a good plan," the admiral commented, looking at the layout with a critical eye.

"There's also plenty of room here for you, sir. If you want it." Steve sprang his surprise on them all at once. "I have some preliminary plans for a home on the edge of the cul de sac with a big backyard and a pool even larger than the one you currently have." He took out some folded papers from his back pocket and handed them to the admiral. They were plans. Small scale because of the small paper, but they could get the general idea. And he had one more thing to show them. "If you'll follow me, there's something else you should see."

Steve set off through the trees, knowing exactly where he was headed. The family lagged behind, each trying to get a look at the papers he'd given the admiral, but they were following. Trisha skipped to catch up with him, a questioning smile on her face.

"You've been planning this?" she asked.

"For a while. The minute I realized where your family lived, I had this idea. And then, when I got here and saw the conditions... All that surveillance. Well, I'm surprised you can live like that. This is an option that will allow your family to thrive without a dozen foreign agents watching their every move. It's better for them, and it's better for the country and the Spec Ops guys your father runs if spies aren't able to see his comings and goings. Believe me, they would never be able to penetrate this neighborhood once it's finished and everyone has moved in."

"That's amazing," she whispered, following him. She was looking at him and he realized the moment she scented what he'd brought her there to see. She sniffed the air and turned her head to look in front of them through the screen of trees. "Is that what I think it is?"

A smile played over her lips as they broke through the last row of trees and stood on the bank of a small river, complete with a new wooden dock and large boat tied to it.

"Oh, wow."

The admiral came up beside on the other side of Steve, the rest of the family stopping on the small rise that led down to the water. Everyone had various expressions of joy on their faces and Steve knew he'd done good.

"River access," the admiral observed. "Nice." That one word from the stoic older man meant more than gushing squeals of joy from a teenage girl. Steve knew the admiral was impressed.

"Would you like a tour? I arranged for the boat to be here. It belongs to a friend and she was happy to let us use it if you want to get a good gauge for exactly where we are in relation to the Rio Grande."

The admiral didn't wait. He started down the bank, his expression fixed on the water. Trisha took Steve's hand and leaned up to kiss his cheek. "You've got him hooked," she whispered. "It won't take much to reel him in." She was laughing as she stepped back and tugged him along to follow after the rest of the family. Her brothers were already on the boat, checking things over.

They spent the day on the water, enjoying the picnic his friend had thoughtfully packed for them. Jim and Rick even stripped to their skivvies and jumped into the river, disappearing for a nice long reconnoiter. They came back an hour later, all smiles, though they waited to report what they'd found to their dad until they'd returned to the building site.

The report was good. Clear, healthy waters and easy access to the Rio Grande not too far away. From there, they could get to the Gulf of Mexico if they wanted. It was a good mode of travel, and possible escape route, for a family that had an affinity for water.

"Okay, Redstone, you've made us an offer it would be almost impossible to refuse," the admiral said as they left the boat and headed back toward the site of the future housing development through the woods. "What would it take for us to get that house built? How much?"

Steve knew he had him, but the next few minutes would clinch it. "Actually, sir, I've been authorized to offer you the house free and clear, if you'll agree to certain conditions."

The admiral stopped short as they cleared the trees and were back at the building site. "What's the catch?"

"Nothing too bad, sir. It's just that these kinds of developments need a leader. You may have noticed the way our Clan is structured. There are Alphas over each group but they all answer ultimately to my brother. We've found that sort of arrangement works best for mixed neighborhoods like this will be. But of the groups that want to live here, there is not one Alpha we think is strong enough to rule them all. That's why nobody has moved in yet. We can't begin populating the neighborhood until we have a strong leader to oversee it all. Grif and I think that could be you, sir."

"But I'm not a shifter," the admiral protested, but Steve could see the wheels turning in the older man's agile mind.

"Dominance isn't always about what kind of animal you can turn into. In your case, it's about raw magical power and the strength of your will. And your character, of course. Strength alone is not enough. The power must be headed in the right direction, if you get my meaning. You serve the Light, sir. It's clear to us all who have served under you. Any shifters or Others who want to live in this neighborhood must also serve the Light. We won't compromise on that. Our communities are on the side of the Lady and we all stand against evil. Others out there aren't so picky, but for us and the communities we build, that's a necessity."

"As it should be." The admiral nodded and looked over the site. "I still have my duties to the military. That comes first until I retire."

"Yes, sir. And if you moved here, you'd still be close to the air support of Loughlin Air Force Base. You'd also have river access to the Gulf. Your duties to the community would take only a small portion of your time and they'd all know your responsibility to the military would take precedence at times. Frankly, a lot of the shifters who will be living here either work on the base or have family members currently serving. It'll be a hybrid military-shifter neighborhood for the most part, which I think might appeal to you. And…there's no way outside surveillance would get past any of them long enough to keep an eye on you. You'd be free of the watchers to live in peace and use your abilities whenever you wish."

The admiral looked over at him, meeting Steve's gaze with a bit of wonder. "You're offering me freedom," the older man whispered.

Steve nodded, a little choked up at the magnitude of the moment. The admiral was silent, clearly thinking hard, judging by the way his expression changed.

"No wonder my daughter fell for you," he finally said, surprising Steve. "Freedom to be ourselves is something me and my children have rarely enjoyed." His voice grew stronger as he started walking again. "How soon can the house be ready?"

Steve went back to Las Vegas, and Trisha followed him soon after. They lived together at his house for the few months it took to build her parents' new home in Texas, visiting often. Plans were made and the wedding date was set. They held the ceremony on the riverbank behind her parents' new house at sunset and had the reception in the backyard. Shifters of all kinds showed up to help celebrate, as well as Trisha's human friends.

Molly was in heaven when Jed Robinson decided to fly in for the wedding with the Redstone brothers. Magnus made his own way there, bringing Miranda as his date to the nighttime reception. The gift Miranda brought was an antique. A lovely baroque vase for the home she and Steve would build together.

They still hadn't settled on where exactly they were going to live, but Trisha knew wherever they ended up, as long as they were together, she was home.

# ABOUT THE AUTHOR

Bianca D'Arc has run a laboratory, climbed the corporate ladder in the shark-infested streets of lower Manhattan, studied and taught martial arts, and earned the right to put a whole bunch of letters after her name, but she's always enjoyed writing more than any of her other pursuits. She grew up and still lives on Long Island, where she keeps busy with an extensive garden, several aquariums full of very demanding fish, and writing her favorite genres of paranormal, fantasy and sci-fi romance.

Bianca loves to hear from readers and can be reached through Twitter (@BiancaDArc), Facebook (BiancaDArcAuthor) or through the various links on her website.

## WELCOME TO THE D'ARC SIDE…
## WWW.BIANCADARC.COM

# OTHER BOOKS BY BIANCA D'ARC

## *Now Available*

*Brotherhood of Blood*
One & Only
Rare Vintage
Phantom Desires
Sweeter Than Wine
Forever Valentine
Wolf Hills

*Tales of the Were*
Lords of the Were
Inferno

*Tales of the Were – The Others*
Rocky
Slade

*Tales of the Were – Redstone Clan*
Grif
Red

*Guardians of the Dark*
Half Past Dead
Once Bitten, Twice Dead
A Darker Shade of Dead
The Beast Within
Dead Alert

*Gifts of the Ancients*
Warrior's Heart

*String of Fate:* Cat's Cradle

*Dragon Knights*
Maiden Flight
The Dragon Healer
Border Lair
Master at Arms
The Ice Dragon
Prince of Spies
Wings of Change
FireDrake
Dragon Storm
Keeper of the Flame

*Resonance Mates*
Hara's Legacy
Davin's Quest
Jaci's Experiment
Grady's Awakening

*Jit'Suku Chronicles*
*Arcana:* King of Swords
*Arcana:* King of Cups
*Arcana:* King of Clubs
End of the Line
*Sons of Amber:* Ezekiel
*Sons of Amber:* Michael

*StarLords:* Hidden Talent

*Print Anthologies*
Ladies of the Lair
I Dream of Dragons Vol. 1
Brotherhood of Blood
Caught by Cupid

# OTHER BOOKS BY BIANCA D'ARC
*(continued)*

### *Coming Soon*

*Dragon Knights*
The Ice Dragon
*Print Re-release: November 5, 2013*

*Dragon Knights*
Prince of Spies
*Print Re-release: December 3, 2013*

*Brotherhood of Blood*
Wolf Quest
*eBook Release: December 10, 2013*
*Print Release: Fall 2014*

*Dragon Knights*
FireDrake
*Print Re-release: January 7, 2014*

*Tales of the Were - Redstone Clan*
Magnus
*Early 2014*

*Dragon Knights*
Dragon Storm
*Print Re-release: February 4, 2014*

*Dragon Knights*
Keeper of the Flame
*Print Re-release: March 4, 2014*

*Resonance Mates*
Harry's Sacrifice
*eBook Release: March 11, 2014*
*Print Release: Winter 2014*

*Tales of the Were - Redstone Clan*
Bobcat
*Spring 2014*

*Tales of the Were - Redstone Clan*
Matt
*Summer 2014*

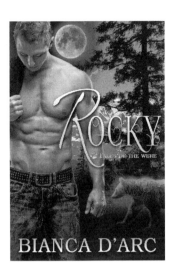

## TALES OF THE WERE – THE OTHERS
## ROCKY
## BY BIANCA D'ARC

*On the run from her husband's killers, there is only one man who can help her now... her Rock.*

Maggie is on the run from those who killed her husband nine months ago. She knows the only one who can help her is Rocco, a grizzly shifter she knew in her youth. She arrives on his doorstep in labor with twins. Magical, shapeshifting, bear cub twins destined to lead the next generation of werecreatures in North America.

Rocky is devastated by the news of his Clan brother's death, but he cannot deny the attraction that has never waned for the small human woman who stole his heart a long time ago. Rocky absented himself from her life when she chose to marry his childhood friend, but the years haven't changed the way he feels for her.

And now there are two young lives to protect. Rocky will do everything in his power to end the threat to the small family and claim them for himself. He knows he is the perfect Alpha to teach the cubs as they grow into their power... if their mother will let him love her as he has always longed to do.

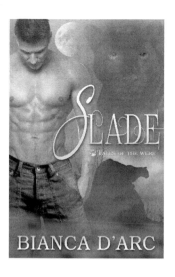

# TALES OF THE WERE – THE OTHERS
## SLADE
## BY BIANCA D'ARC

*The fate of all shifters rests on his broad shoulders, but all he can think of is her.*

Slade is a warrior and spy sent to Nevada to track a brutal murderer before the existence of all shifters is revealed to a world not ready to know.

Kate is a priestess serving the large community of shifters that have gathered around the Redstone cougars. When their matriarch is murdered and the scene polluted by dark magics, she knows she must help the enigmatic man sent to track the killer.

Together, Slade and Kate find not one but two evil mages that they alone can neutralize. Slade finds it hard to keep his hands off his sexy new partner, the cougars are out for blood, and the killers have an even more sinister plan in mind.

Can Kate somehow keep her hands to herself when the most attractive man she's ever met makes her want to throw caution to the wind? And can Slade do his job and save the situation when he's finally found a woman who can make him purr?

# TALES OF THE WERE – REDSTONE CLAN
## GRIF
### BY BIANCA D'ARC

Griffon Redstone is the eldest of five brothers and the leader of one of the most influential shifter Clans in North America. He seeks solace in the mountains, away from the horrific events of the past months, for both himself and his young sister. The deaths of their older sister and mother have hit them both very hard.

Lindsey Tate is human, but very aware of the werewolf Pack that lives near her grandfather's old cabin. She's come to right a wrong her grandfather committed against the Pack and salvage what's left of her family's honor—if the wolves will let her. Mostly, they seem intent on running her out of town on a rail.

But the golden haired stranger, Grif, comes to her rescue more than once. He stands up for her against the wolf Pack and then helps her fix the old generator at the cabin. When she performs a ceremony she expects will end in her death, the shifter deity has other ideas. Thrown together by fate, neither of them can deny their deep attraction, but will an old enemy tear them apart?

*Warning: Cats are frisky and they get up to all sorts of naughtiness, including a frenzy-induced multi-partner situation that might be a little intense for some readers.*

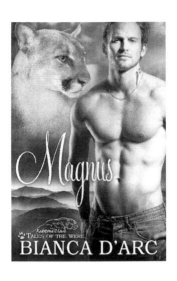

## TALES OF THE WERE – REDSTONE CLAN
## MAGNUS
## BY BIANCA D'ARC

Magnus Redstone is the middle of five brothers. As a result, he's always had a little bit of a hard time forging his own identity. While he excels at martial arts, he didn't want to be a soldier like Grif and Steve, his two older brothers. He also doesn't have time for practical jokes like the younger two, Bob and Matt. No, Mag is probably the most serious of the brothers and he always has been. The only real moment when he threw caution to the wind was when he met one very special lady. A lady with fangs...

*Coming Early 2014 in eBook and Print*

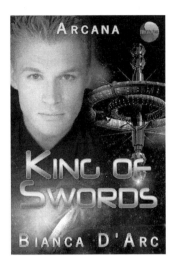

# KING OF SWORDS
## BY BIANCA D'ARC
### *Arcana, Book 1*

David is a newly retired special ops soldier, looking to find his way in an unfamiliar civilian world. His first step is to visit an old friend, the owner of a bar called *The Rabbit Hole* on a distant space station. While there, he meets an intriguing woman who holds the keys to his future.

Adele has a special ability, handed down through her family. Adele can sometimes see the future. She doesn't know exactly why she's been drawn to the space station where her aunt deals cards in a bar that caters to station workers and ex-military. She only knows that she needs to be there. When she meets David, sparks of desire fly between them and she begins to suspect that he is part of the reason she traveled halfway across the galaxy.

Pirates gas the inhabitants of the station while Adele and David are safe inside a transport tube and it's up to them to repel the invaders. Passion flares while they wait for the right moment to overcome the alien threat and retake the station. But what good can one retired soldier and a civilian do against a ship full of alien pirates?

Made in the USA
San Bernardino, CA
26 December 2013